CULLING A
Miracle

Michelle Janene

Sacramento, CA

Strong Tower Press
PO Box 293632
Sacramento, CA 95829
http://strongtowerpress.com

Publishers Note: This is a work of fiction.
Names, characters, places, and incidents are either
products of the author's imagination or used factiously.
All characters are fictional, and any
Similarity to any person living or dead is entirely coincidental.

Cover Art by: Whetstone Designs
Editing by: Susan S. Sage
Images: Mortal and Pestle 123 RF, ID# 25304467, Thanarat Boonmee
Swirl - seamartini Image ID : 11497604, 123RF Stock Photo
Cover: couple ID: 25849327, Sergejs Rahunoks, 123RF Stock Photo
Fort ID: 31879174, Andrey Andronov, 123RF Stock Photo
Herbs ID: 79491111, Natallia Khlapushyna, 123RF Stock Photo
ISBN: 978-1-942320-25-8

… For I am fearfully and wonderfully made…
Psalms 139:14 ESV

In all of history past

Or the unseen future

There has never been and will never be anyone with

your

DNA

Skills

Talents

Experiences

*For we are his workmanship, created in Christ Jesus for
good works,
which God prepared beforehand, that we should walk in
them.*
Ephesians 2:10 ESV

And remember to choose love.

Chapter 1

"You're covered in blood!" Bethany jerked her son out of the path and glowered.

Father Abel made the sign of the cross. "What evil have you been about?"

"Mum look, Esmeralda killed someone. She's all bloody." Little Selah hid her face in her mother's skirts.

"Oh, goose feathers to the highest heavens." Esmeralda waved her arms; the dried blood now caked up to her elbows. "'Tis naught more than goat's blood."

"'Tis a heresy to worship the dark one." Father Abel sputtered as he stumbled back a step.

Esmeralda continued walking through the center of town without slowing. "I am a follower of the Lord Most High, Father, as well you know." A grin pulled at her lips as she spun to look at them while continuing to walk backwards. "Peter's doe just delivered her first kid and he had to be cut from his mother." Esmeralda spun with a skip and shouted over her shoulder. "And they are both hale."

More of the good folk of Flatwell dodged from her path as Esmeralda bounced down the lane. The only thing to dampen her mood was the dog dung she'd been unable to avoid squishing between her toes as she dodged an angry fist waving from Travers, the blacksmith.

Long after the last homes on the west side of village, Esmeralda entered the woods that lay within the walls of their town. She kept to the well-worn path she could follow in the deepest hours of a moonless night. The forest animals didn't scurry to their dens, or scamper off in fear. It was just Esz, another one of the wild creatures who lived in their forest home.

"MeeMa?" Esmeralda sang out as the tiny hut came into view. "MeeMa, you are never going to guess my adventures of this day." She drew back the leather flap from over the opening and savored the cool earthen floor. But the dark hovel lay empty.

"What is all the caterwaulin' about?" MeeMa padded around her hut from her herb garden. Her slender fame, covered in a soft brown kirtle, blended in with the surrounding foliage. "Oh, Eszy, child. Ya're a fright. Come, come let us get ya cleaned up. What mischief have ya gotten into now?"

"No mischief. I promise." She let herself be herded toward the stream where a tub of water sat. MeeMa worked to scrub her arms clean. "Peter's goat delivered."

"And what about a kid coming into the world causes ya lookin' like a warrior returned from battle?"

Esmeralda could hardly stand still. "The kid was all turned about inside. Wouldn't come out like God intended. The doe was a wailin' and Peter yelled for me come to help. I held the mum still and he carefully sliced open her belly. He pulled out the little lad and placed him on my lap then sewed up the mum with some of the finest stitches I ever have seen. You would've been proud of him."

Her arms cleaned, MeeMa waved for Esmeralda to raise them as she continued to recount her tale without a breath. Her stained overdress whisked over her head leaving her in her tattered and stained chemise.

"Never seen anything like it. The doe stood and suckled her kid as though it was any other birthing."

"Mothers are resilient, Eszy. Ya've helped me deliver enough babes in Flatwell to know such."

"But you haven't ever cut a babe free from the womb."

MeeMa stood staring at her for a moment. The wet overdress created a puddle at her feet. "No, no I haven't done that, though may have saved the miller's wife and babe had I thought of it." She pushed a strand of wispy gray hair from her leathery face with her forearm. "I pray ya never have call ta use such knowledge, but the good Lord has provided it to ya, so mind it well."

Esmeralda spun and danced about in the clearing beside the stream as MeeMa fussed over her garment. The new stains would only be added to the old. On one of her spins, she caught MeeMa staring at her.

"Ya remind me of yar mum, dancing around like a fairy sprite."

"Tell me about her, please."

"Oh, child, ya have done heard all me tales a hundred score now."

"Please." Esmeralda clutched her hands to her chest and did one tight spin.

MeeMa's blue eyes almost disappeared in her wrinkles. Her gaze shifted off toward the town. "A fine woman, yar mum. Always treated me with kindness. Brought me any food she could spare and didn't take to no one calling me a witch." A smile pulled at the corner of her lips. "She danced and twirled about like ya did just now when she came to tell me the most fetching lad in all the realm had asked for her hand."

MeeMa's gaze shifted back to her, "And ya came along about a winter later. Same russet hair and emerald eyes as yar mum's. That's why they named ya Esmeralda. Oh, how Sariad loved ya, child." Her gaze slid off to the distance again. "Sore I am, my herbs were no match for the fever that stole her from ya too young."

Esmeralda laid her hand on MeeMa's arm. "I know you did everything for her. Father told me. You loved her."

MeeMa patted her hand. "That I did, child. That I did."

"But then the good Lord saw it fitting to call yar fine father home too." MeeMa tossed her head sending her gray waves to fluttering.

"Doesn't seem right to leave such a sweet child all on her own in the world."

"I'm not alone. I have you."

MeeMa clucked her tongue. "Without Sariad speaking on me behalf, ya know the town has labeled me a witch." She waved Esmeralda back toward the hut. "Ya have done yarself no favors by spending yar hours with me, child."

As MeeMa tottered, Esmeralda twirled around her. She may have been too old to do so, but Esz never cared much for what others thought of her. If she did, she wouldn't be here with MeeMa. "But you have taught me herbs, teas, ointments, treatments for mending bone, and wounds."

"And ya pester any traveler who comes to town to learn of any other treatments they may know." She chuckled as she led the way into her home and draped the soggy overdress across a log near the hearth. "Yar desire to gain knowledge of the healing arts is like a gnawing hunger, akin to that of a bear after wakin' from his winter's rest."

MeeMa stirred the stewpot hanging over the flames releasing wafts of rich meat that drove out the lingering traces of dirt and moldy thatch. The small hut held little. A lopsided tiny table with two mismatched, rickety stools, a longer worktable where they prepared their herbs, and MeeMa's straw palate in the corner made the room feel cramped. Esz had to be mindful of the low ceiling beam that MeeMa passed under with ease.

Esmeralda slid an errant strand that had come loose from the plait behind her ear and scrutinized the collection of herbs waiting on the worktable. "You found chamomile."

"Yes, yes, the last for this season. Hope 'tis enough to see Margaret through the winter with her headaches."

"Do you wish me to boil the flax seeds?"

MeeMa patted her on the arm. "I think ya have done enough for one day, child. Come sit. Eat." She waved at the stool Esmeralda always used. With their cups full on the tiny table and MeeMa perched on the other stool, they bowed their head for grace.

"Our precious Heavenly Father," MeeMa's voice was strong and full of awe. "We give Thee thanks for all the bounty of Thy hand. For the food to sustain us and the herbs and knowledge to mend us. May we always bring Thee praise by the work of our hands. Amen."

"Amen."

With their cups half emptied, MeeMa paused to stare at her. MeeMa tapped her wooden spoon staring at it as she spoke to Esz. "I tell ya again, Eszy, 'tis high time we find a man to take yar hand."

Esmeralda whisked her own spoon through the air waving her off. "I am two score and one. Far beyond the desirable age to be wed. And we both know well; no man of worth would consider me. They think me odd, MeeMa. Possessed of the devil at worst and addled at best."

"Yar the brightest of all in this town, Eszy. Nay let any speak against ya."

Laughter danced from Esmeralda. "Mayhaps the long missing king will order every town to have a proper healer to maintain his people's good health."

"Ya dream for the impossible."

Esmeralda let a smirk pull at her lips. "Well, we could always pray for selection in the Culling."

MeeMa spit on the floor and shot a string of Hail Father's at the thatch. "Never do I want to hear ya wish such ill on yarself or any other maid, Esmeralda." The spoon wagged at her nose again. "Thou shall not court evil."

Chapter 2

"Esz? Oh, you useless girl, where are you?"

"I'm here." Esmeralda stepped from the shadow of the stable, arms crossed. "If I am so very useless then I can only conclude you no longer require my tea." She turned and started to walk away. "As I have much to do this day, I thank you for not making me wait any longer…"

Dinah grabbed her arm and jerked Esmeralda back toward the shadows. Releasing her almost as quickly, Dinah wiped her hand on her skirt. "Stop it, Esz. You know well Mum requires the calming." She rested her arms on the top rail of the corral and looked at the horses milling about inside. "You just don't know what it's like to be under threat of the Culling."

"I am only three summers older than you and still a maiden." Esmeralda leaned her back against the rails and huffed. "They could take me as easily as you."

"How many times have you been offered?"

"Twice, but the first I was far too young. They never take the very young."

Dinah nodded. "True, but now…" She rubbed her arms as if chilled though the sun was bright and it was warm even in the shadows.

"Surely *you* do not lack prospective matches. It isn't as if you have the orphan's taint on your name."

"No one cares that your parents are dead, Esz." Her voice dropped to a whisper. "It is that you conduct yourself with the witch."

Esz growled low and deep. "If I didn't conduct myself with Old Widow Mia, and if she and I didn't scour the woods and glens for the herbs, dry them, grind and mix them, where would you and your dear pious mother get your tea? MeeMa has done naught but tend the sick and injured, and you scorn her for the knowledge that aids."

"I only say what is well known about the town."

"Other towns have healers—apothecaries even. They are respected members of a healthy community. Dinah, just because Flatwell is full of superstitious ninnies doesn't mean you have to be one of them. You have known me all your life. Have I ever done anything to harm anyone?"

"Nay, you haven't, but you could, and we would never suspect it."

"You have as much opportunity to fall to sin as I, but you don't see me going about blaming you before you have acted." Esmeralda pulled a pouch cinched with string from the satchel slung across her body. "Your mum's tea. May she drink it in good health."

"Thank you. Lord willing, Mum and Da will see me wed before the next Culling."

"It has been almost three years. Mayhaps the Culling with its unwashed men won't return again."

"Or they could come tomorrow." Dinah scurried off.

Esmeralda rounded the stable and ambled into town. She noted the men and women who moved to the other side of the lane rather than risk bumping shoulders with her. Her garments may be tattered and stained, but these same good folks, who wouldn't share the street with her, also never thought to offer payment for the remedies she and MeeMa provided. She bathed regularly, but there was not the coin for cloth or new clothes. She squared her shoulders, head held high, and dared each person to look her in the eye and acknowledge her. Few did. And she stifled the shriek crawling at the back of her throat.

A wagon in front of the tavern caught her eye. She skipped ahead, heedless of the people scrambling from her path. The reeds covering the tavern's floor tickled her toes, and the heady odor of men and ale made her nose wrinkle.

"No women—oh, Esz 'tis you." Rizard, the tavern owner, returned to his tasks. He'd long ago given up trying keeping her out.

Esz passed the rows of long tables on either side of the central aisle. The dark wood tables and walls gave the room a heaviness that always made her breath catch. Flickering lamp light cast the few patrons in a sickly yellow light and made specter-like shadows dance about the room. Esz tossed off the foreboding sensations as she moved deeper into the room. She knelt on a bench and leaned on her forearms as they rested on the tabletop. Neal, the traveling merchant, put down his tankard and smiled at her.

"Didn't take ya long to discover me, lass."

"Did you bring it?"

He tilted his head and considered her. "Good-day to ya too, lass."

"'Tis a very good day 'cause you have returned and you probably brought me ginger." Esmeralda gave him her biggest smile.

"And what are you willing to pay for me ginger? I'm a businessman. Can't go giving away me merchandise. 'Tis bad business." He winked at her.

Esmeralda laughed. They had played this game since she was a child when she would place her feet on top of his and they'd dance down the center aisle of the tavern. She stood and curtsied low. "May I have the honor of this dance, sir?"

Neal rose and bowed deep. "M'lady." He set his dance frame like any nobleman she had ever imagined and Esmeralda stepped into it. He placed his left hand low on her back, and she put her right palm on his shoulder. Their other hands clasped gently as Neal kept a respectable distance between their bodies. They nodded at the same time and started the steps of the simple dance, spinning and sliding down the length of the tavern and back. Without any music, they followed the rhythm they had set and repeated over countless years.

Neal was not a tall man. Over the years Esz had grown to over take his meager height by a few finger widths. With her gaze above his forehead, Esz noted that Neal's hair was continuing to thin. When he leaned forward to assure he didn't step on her bare toes, she saw the crown of his head looked blistered and angry red. "I can give you an ointment for the burn of the sun," Esmeralda said as they finished and returned to the table.

"You are ever kind, lass." He produced a pouch much like she had given Dinah, only three times larger as he bowed again. "Your goods, m'lady."

She squealed and stooped to peck his check with a kiss. "Thank you, Neal." She exchanged the pouch of ginger with a palm-sized jar of ointment. "Each morning put a thin layer over your scalp where 'tis burned. And you should procure a hat." She skipped from the tavern.

A glance to the east showed a dark horizon over the town's high crenelated wall, and an ill wind blew. Esmeralda stifled a shiver.

Chapter 3

"How is your mum, Dinah?" Esz asked two days later.

The blonde-headed girl glanced about her to see who watched her talking to the witch's apprentice. Moving a little forward she spoke but didn't look at Esmeralda. "The tea has served her, but she will not need it any longer if the negotiations with the miller and his son go well."

"They seek to match you with Vin?" The lanky lad was a season younger than Dinah, and not at all attractive. All long spindly limbs and a long face. Still, Esmeralda had to admit she would have found a way to love him if Vin had asked for her hand.

"Yes, but Abigail's father seeks a match as well." Dinah nibbled on the tip of her index finger. "I don't know what Mum and I will do if Vin doesn't choose me."

Esmeralda shrugged and turned. "The Lord will provide."

"Well, He better do so soon. *They* could return at any moment."

"Taste and see that the Lord is good."

"Esz?"

Esmeralda stopped and looked back.

"You have straw in your hair."

She ran her hand over her head and down her plait, pulling out a couple of wayward stalks. Dinah had disappeared when she looked up to thank her.

Esmeralda continued down the lane on the outer edges of the south part of town to the small house beside the tannery. The pungent odor of drying hides and tannins made her cough against the lump spouting up to the back of her throat. Keeping out of sight, she skirted the tanner and followed the wails of the tanner's wee daughter to the far side of their home. She lay in a basket as her mum, Loral, hung the laundry.

"Esz." Loral jumped and clutched the tunic she held to her chest. Her gazed darted about. "You can nay be here. If Barid were to see you…"

Esmeralda dropped the pouch of calming herbs in the baby's basket and handed Loral another before turning.

"Ya filthy witch!" Barid raised his sword in the air and stomped toward her. "I told ya I'd run ya through if'n I ever seen ya near me family."

Clutching her satchel close, Esmeralda dashed in the opposite direction. Barid roared and his good-wife screamed. Esmeralda squeezed between two houses that nearly touched. Barely enough room for her, Barid couldn't follow. He bellowed curses and raced out of sight. Her satchel caught, jerking her back. She pulled it free. The tanner's furious shout came toward her. He had rounded one of the houses to cut off her escape.

Esmeralda looked up to the low rooftops. She braced her hands, followed by her feet against each house, and shimmied her way up. She pulled herself onto one of the thatch tops just as Barid thrust his sword into the narrow space.

He gasped. "She's disappeared! Witch. I tell ya she's a witch."

Esmeralda lay panting on the rough thatch. Her eyes squeezed tight against the tears. Would she ever find a place to belong?

Esmeralda dropped to the ground an hour later. She brushed off her hands and turned toward MeeMa's hut.

"There she is! The witch."

Fists clenched at her side until her nails drew blood, Esmeralda whirled. "I am no witch."

"Esmeralda, you must explain how you vanished before Barid's very eyes."

"Fie, Father Abel. Only an imbecile would believe any human had the power to vanish." She thrust her hands out in front of the growing crowd. "While that fool ran around the houses, I climbed to the roof." Her hands and feet were covered with cuts and scratches. She next yanked bits of thatch from her hair and dress flicking it at Barid. "I lay on roof waiting for this buffoon to stop his caterwauling so I could return home."

She turned on the tanner now, bloody finger wagging in the air. "And only a heartless cur would allow his babe to wail until exhausted for the hatred of a woman who wanted nothing more than to ease the child's discomfort."

"Why you filthy—" Barid drew his sword again.

A long low bellow of a the horn called out from the top of the wall.

Women shrieked.

Girls sobbed.

Another time of Culling had returned.

"Pray you are taken or I shall see you burned." Barid said shoving her toward the gate.

Chapter 4

Each maiden of marrying age responded when the town elder called her name. Together the maidens left their sobbing mothers and cursing fathers within the gate and went to present themselves. Esz stood stoic surrounded by sniveling girls.

Nearly threescore had walked through the gate to stand side by side a few feet outside the wall. They trembled in a long line facing the warriors outside. Sisters clung to one another. Friends held hands. Esmeralda stood tall, alone.

Dinah chewed her finger as she sniffled. "Only another day. Couldn't they have waited one more day?"

Three black-clad, scruffy warriors rode forward. Without word or challenge they entered the village. Esz had heard from her earliest remembering that if the men were to find any maidens hidden within the city, the rest of the barbarians would charge in and slaughter every male and take *all* the women, but Esz never heard for sure that these bandits hurt anyone. Flatwell knew better. All of the girls who fit the requirements stood outside the gate. Their families stood on the battlements above. Watching. Praying. If any prayed over her, it was in hopes she would be the one taken.

When the three warriors returned from the town, one lone rider, who'd waited with the remaining warriors outside, came forward and stepped off his warhorse. The great roan pawed the earth as his master came to the first girl in the line. His fists clenched and unclenched repeatedly as he asked, "Tell me your name."

In turn, each maiden said her name. Some through tears. Others whispered. All looked to their toes.

"Dinah, m'lord."

Esmeralda would not shy away from this man who came to steal one of them. Through the unwashed, uncombed hair and the unruly beard little of the man's face showed. His head tipped, moving the strands from his eyes, which were the color of the blade at his hip. His gaze held hers.

"Esmeralda."

He lingered. One heartbeat. Then another.

She would not be the first to look away.

He continued down the line, dismissing some to flee back to their mums. Their numbers dwindled by half. He made his way back down the line. "Tell me of your family."

As the girls cowered before the man, each told of those she would be leaving behind.

"There is no one who claims me," Esmeralda said. "Only a kindly shunned widow will even mark my absence."

His shoulders sagged a mite. His gaze softened.

He dismissed all but four. Dinah, Abigail and her sister, and Esmeralda.

He backed several steps to consider them all together, his fists continuing to clench and unclench.

"I'm frightened," Dinah choked.

"We don't know what happens to the women they take." Esmeralda brushed her hand against the trembling girl's.

"But they never return."

The warrior waved Esmeralda forward.

"Please tell MeeMa what has become of me," she whispered to Dinah. She stepped to him on strong sure strides. Still staring boldly.

"Will you come with me willingly, Esmeralda?"

"Aye."

He waved the others back to the gate and swept out a hand toward his men for them to follow. The dark horses parted to reveal a solid white mare. "Can you ride?"

"Has been a while."

He nodded. "Let me assist you." He helped her into the saddle. "I am Tiobald. I, and these men, will watch over you and keep you safe." His men surrounded her and Tiobald lead them toward the east.

She dared a glance back at the town she would never see again. The gates were shut tight. No one stood atop the walls to wave farewell. No birds sang. Only the creaking of leather and the metallic rustle of chain mail filled the glen.

Chapter 5

Fears bombarded her thoughts in torrents as they rode in silence. What did they intend to do with her at journey's end? Would they sacrifice her in some horrid pagan ritual? Did they intend to set upon her and assault her—each taking his turn until she expired? Did they take her to be sold to a distant king?

All these possible outcomes were talked about amongst her people since the Culling began before she was born. But no one truly knew what became of their women. Each had ridden off never to return.

She wondered if Dinah would indeed venture out to the hut in the woods and tell MeeMa of her fate.

"Taste and see that the Lord is good." She had said to Dinah just the other day. Esmeralda closed her eyes as the horse swayed lazily beneath her. *I will sing unto the Lord, for He hath dealt bountifully with me.* She let the verse from Psalms echo in her heart.

The movement stopped and her eyes popped open. After riding through the day, the sun sat low on the horizon peeking through the thick trees that towered over them. The men moved away and dismounted. Tiobald approached and reached up to help her.

His arms were massive—larger around than her thighs. His hands— twice the size of hers. His power evident in the ease with which he lowered her to the ground. But when her traitorous legs betrayed her, the tenderness that embraced and supported her stilled her heart.

"Forgive me, Esmeralda. The ride has been too long for one thus inexperienced as you. It was imperative we reach this glen before nightfall."

His words were a soft caress on her frayed nerves. She looked up and searched his face for some clue as to what would become of her in this isolated place.

He smiled—or at least she thought he did. His thick beard made it hard to know for sure. "Come walk with me for a moment and you will feel better." As they strolled away from the others who seemed busy unburdening their horses, Tiobald's arm circled her waist and supported her. "Esmeralda, let me explain why we have come and taken you from your home."

A shiver raced through her before she could contain it.

"You have nothing to fear. When I am finished, if you do not wish to continue, we will see you taken to a town where you will be welcomed. No one will force you to do anything you do not wish."

She stopped and looked up at him. Her brows pulled together. This was not what she'd expected.

"Keep walking. It will ease the tightness in your legs." Once they were moving, he told his story. His voice was rich and soothing, and somehow made up for the ripe smell emanating from him. "We are from a small hamlet to your east called Rustshade. Three score years ago a blight fell upon our community. Our women began to lose their babes before they drew their first breath. Not long after that, our women also died in childbirth." He glanced over his shoulder at the men behind them. "We are the last of our people. When our women were gone, we went in search of others. First, we tried wooing women to marry, but soon word spread of the deaths and none would come. We were forced to collect them in a more demanding fashion. But all were given the choice I am giving you now. Many accepted, all have died but the last few who have yet to attempt to bring their babes forth."

He stopped and his silver eyes captured hers. They were moist with unshed tears. "I am one of the last born in Rustshade. The last to seek a bride. You are the last woman ever to be taken from any village. What I ask is an almost certain death sentence until a way can be found to heal our women and save our babes. Every effort is being made, but—" he raked his hand through his hair pushing it back from his face, "know that you will be greatly honored, well treated, and deeply loved should you agree to accept my hand." He looked at her expectantly.

A marriage proposal and a death sentence in the same breath had not been what she bargained on when she agreed to come with this man. Honored, treated well, even loved—could she really gain all her heart's desires with one simple *yes*. A thought niggled at the back of her tongue. "I have some knowledge in the healing arts. My people called me a witch, but mayhaps I was meant for your people."

Tiobald blinked. "You would agree—" his words sputtered and faltered.

"Is this not why you brought me here?"

He nodded, his eyes crinkling up at the corners revealing the smile his unruly beard tried to hide. "I didn't dare dream you would agree."

"I do agree."

He took her hands, engulfing them in his. But it was his that trembled. "I cannot tell you my joy. Come, all has been prepared." He turned her back toward the others. "A private place for you to bathe and change has been arranged." He pointed to a sliver of white coming through the trees. "I will meet you here when you are ready."

He turned but only made it a step before she stopped him. "Tiobald? Why me?"

He stepped close and brushed her cheek with the back of a finger. It was warm yet rough and sent a hum over her skin. "Because you were brave, and beautiful, and—willing."

He left her standing there. The evening air chilling the spot his finger had warmed.

Chapter 6

Tiobald's men stood guard with their backs to a wooden frame draped in fabric straddling a bubbling stream. Inside, a neatly bundled pile of garments waited high on the bank, with towels and soapwort and lavender.

Esmeralda slid into the water to find it a warm spring. She took her time and cleaned thoroughly before donning the new undergarments, chemise, and fine linen overdress. The fabric was soft against her skin. T'was the most luxurious thing she had ever worn, without a tear or stain, and it reached clear to her toes. She secured the belt around her waist, contouring the fabric to match her slender ill-fed frame. Hose were under the dress as well as a pair of supple leather slippers. Though a little big, they were a blessing that brought tears to her eyes.

Using the silver brush provided, she worked the tangles from her hair stroke by stroke until her russet hair fell dry and smooth around her shoulders. Checking her reflection in the water, she wondered if Tiobald really believed she was beautiful, or if he would have said the same to any maiden he selected.

After so long wearing a too short—to the point of being scandalous —garment, having to pick up her hem made her smile. She stepped from the enclosure and made her way back to the spot Tiobald said he would wait. The men milled about. A few were now clean-shaven, most had trimmed their breads and hair. Their tunics were bright and their mood light as they laughed and slapped one another on the shoulder.

As she joined them in the twilight, all eyes turned and a hush again fell over them. They bowed deep, each offering a "m'lady" as she passed. She scanned them looking for Tiobald.

"You are a vision." The voice was familiar but the face was not. The last rays of the sun sparkled in clean black hair, which was now neatly trimmed to just below his collar. His beard was short, hugging the contour of his strong jaw and high cheekbones. His pale red lips were turned up and parted. This man was the finest creature Esmeralda had ever seen. This couldn't be her future husband. But the silver-colored eyes were Tiobald's, and they swept over her from the top of her head to the hem of her gown. A garment the same pale-blue color and weave as his tunic.

He reached out his hand for her. She was sure her heart stopped. But the moment their fingers touched, energy like a lightning strike surged through her and stole her breath.

His meaty fingers laced between hers spreading them wide. He led her to a man whose head was tonsured. His long brown robe brushed the blades of grass at his feet. Tiobald knelt before the monk and guided Esz to her knees beside him. She prayed she wouldn't rise to find grass stains on her beautiful gown.

She looked to Tiobald who smiled at her, and turned to the monk who wore such a scowl it chased her own smile into hiding.

"The conditions of your capture have been fully explained to you?" His voice was sharp and bitter.

"Tiobald has asked for my hand in hopes that I might produce an heir for their people where none has survived before."

"And you willingly except this sentence?"

"Monk, I believe God Himself has brought me to this, my new family, not to die, but to bring life; to find love where there has been none, acceptance where there has been only scorn and rejection, honor where there has been hatred. I am coming home."

The monk huffed and began the rites. "Do you take this woman in sickness and till death?"

"I will." Tiobald's response was strong and possessive, quickening her heart.

"And do you take this man, submitting to him until death, forsaking all others?"

"I will." She hoped she sounded as sure as he had as she squeezed his hand.

"Then in the sight of God, you are husband and wife—until death claims you." The monk turned to leave.

"Do you not intend to bless us?" Esmeralda rocked back to her heels and rose.

"You will find no blessing in the life you have agreed to, child."

"How dare you." She continued though Tiobald's hand tightened on hers. "God blesses all His children. It is not for you to say who is worthy of such gifts. Did not Christ Himself commission His followers, 'Whatsoever thou shalt bind on earth shalt be bound in heaven'? If you do His will, Monk, you will bind us with a blessing and not curse us with your disdain."

The men around her muttered as they shifted their weight from foot to foot.

Esmeralda would not relent. She stared the man down. "Are you not to spread the Good News of the Father's redemption and love—to all and not merely to those you believe deserving? Are we not children of the King? Will you withhold what Christ offered to all—even His betrayer?"

"The Lord bless thee, and keep thee: The Lord make His face shine upon thee, and be gracious unto thee: The Lord lift up His countenance upon thee, and give thee peace." The words were not spoken with joy but resignation. But they were spoken.

Esmeralda closed her eyes and let the blessing wash over her spirit.

The Lord blessed her with a future and not an end when she left Flatwell. He would keep her from the death of those who had gone before her and from the hatred of those she left behind. His face already shone on her. She bathed in the radiance of His love as surely as she had washed her body in the stream. He was gracious to provide a man of fine features and gentle spirit. And she knew God's peace more powerfully than ever before.

When she opened her eyes, the monk was gone. Tiobald stood staring at her, his mouth agape.

Heat flooded her cheeks and for the first time she averted her gaze. "Forgive me."

He pulled her close. One finger raised her chin. His steely eyes sparkled and his mouth danced with mirth. "Is this the fire I have to look forward to?"

The heat rose to blister her face. "I fear what you saw as bravery outside Flatwell's gate, most have called brazen disregard."

He moved closer until their toes touched. His thumb traced her jaw making her breath stutter. "I call it strength and passion." His fingers slide into her hair until he cradled her head. "And it fires my soul." His lips brushed hers—hot and soft. His beard tickled. He captured her lower lip between his.

She rested her hands on his chest as she rose to the tips of her toes, a surprising hunger driving her for more. Muscles rippled under her palms as his other arm encircled her and crushed her to him. His lips devoured hers. He pulled away as if scorched.

The *clank* of a pot. The *thwack* of an ax against wood brought Tiobald's head up, stealing her breath with it. Her legs quaked beneath her and she sagged against him. Heart pulsing in her ears, he hugged her tight for a moment, kissing the top of her head. "Let's get some food in you. Then you should rest. It has been an eventful day."

He had no idea.

Chapter 7

"Good morn, brother." Connin slapped Tiobald on the shoulder. He leaned against the same tree as Tio and his gaze followed the same path to the slumbering woman in the center of two concentric rings of sleeping warriors. "She's a fiery one." A broad smile filled his friend's face. "Looks as though you chose well. She is sure to keep your bed quite warm."

"Don't be crude, Con."

"Still, I'm happy to see you have at last fulfilled your duty."

"You know why I resisted. Why we have all resisted."

"I know you feel it cruel, but we weren't meant to live alone. God can choose to bless us again at any time."

Tio's lips curved. "She's been alone and shunned amongst her people. When I came before them, she stared me down, almost daring me with those green jewels in her skull."

"Fiery."

Tio shook his head. "Nay, it was not anger, nor defiance. 'Twas… strength. An unwavering conviction in the rightness of the matter."

"Then she is truly a good match for you."

"She says she is a healer," Tio whispered.

Connin straightened and looked at him. "Do you think?"

"I pray so."

Esmeralda stirred. She winced and rubbed at her legs as she sat up. Connin slapped him on the shoulder again with a chuckle as Tio made his way to her.

"Good morn, Esmeralda. I apologize again for the long ride." He knelt at her feet.

Her smile was genuine. The gentle curve of her lips reminding him of their softness and warmth. "Good morn, Husband." She giggled at the word. "I never thought to say that." She pointed her toes and the sweet features of her oval face pinched.

"May I?" he reached for her foot and calf. She nodded. As he massaged her knotted calves and flexed her feet in turn, she leaned back on her hands, threw back her head, and hummed a contented whispered moan.

"I know it was not ideal, but I hope you slept well."

Her smile had returned when looked at him again. "Very well. Far warmer here by the fire than a drafty stable loft. To say nothing of the smell." She glanced around. "I've often slept outdoors but never felt this safe."

"I'm sorry your life has been difficult. I hope you are not trading one difficulty for another."

She reached for his hands, and he pulled her to her feet. Her hands again rested on his chest, light as whispers but warm as a mighty blaze. Green eyes searched his face. A smile parted her lips. "Things are looking up. You offer a fresh start. A place where I might make a difference." The tip of her tongue traced her full lips, and she rose bringing them toward his.

Tio's heart lodged in his throat. How could this woman so quickly burrow into his soul? She captured him as he did a rabbit in a snare. On its own, his finger traced the silky skin of her cheek. Her head tilted into his hand and her eyes closed. She trapped his hand between her face and her own hand and breathed deep. Then she turned and kissed his palm.

He pulled away. He couldn't hurt her. Any life with him was a death sentence.

"You look tired. Did you not sleep well?" She snatched up her bag and started rummaging through it. "I can mix you a restorative tea."

He put his hand over hers. "I'm fine. I did not sleep last night."

She snapped straight; her fine red brows drew together.

He offered his hand again, and they walked the remaining kinks out of her legs. "I did not sleep so that I could watch over you."

"But there are so many—"

"A husband must prove he can keep his family safe." The words bit. There was no way for any man in Rustshade to be a good husband *and* protect his family. One would always cost the other.

"Do you plan to never sleep?"

He chuckled. "Yesterday I proved I would protect you. Today I hunt. I will meet you where we will next camp and prove that I will provide for you as well."

She pulled up short and her fist perched on her full hip. "You go into the woods alone, to hunt wild game, with no sleep, to prove you…"

"'Tis tradition. Tomorrow we ride together to prove I can be a good companion." He offered his hand yet again.

This time she hesitated. "Tradition is all fine and good, until it gets someone killed. I don't care to lose any more family, Tiobald." She at last relinquished her hand to him and they moved back to the men where she ate as the othrs began to break camp.

As Tio rode into the woods, he turned and saw her watching. *I don't care to lose any more family either, Esmeralda.*

Chapter 8

The hunt had gone well. Exceedingly well. One might even call it blessed. Within mere hours of parting from Esmeralda and the rest of his guard, Tio had brought down two stags and a boar. He butchered them and put the meat on a litter. Even so, he arrived at their next place to camp before the others. He made three fire pits and roasted the meat as he waited.

As the spits dropped grease into the flames, savory flavors filled the clearing. Tio rested under a nearby tree, his head lulled back. With his eyes closed, memories danced. Green sparkling eyes that captured his gaze and wouldn't let go. Hair, the color of dogwood leaves in the fall, flowed like a glistening stream. Supple lips, hungry to be kissed. The scent of jasmine and lavender danced in his nose so strongly, Tio looked up expecting to see her sitting beside him. His heart sank when she wasn't there. How could his feelings be so strong for a woman he'd only known a day? A woman his love would inevitably kill?

He stood, clenching and unclenching his fists. He scooped up his ax, stomped into the brush, felled a sapling, and chopped it to pieces. Hacking away, he tried his best not to think of the woman who called him husband.

Returning to the fires with an armload of wood, he glanced up. The riders came over the rise. Tio froze waiting to get a glimpse of her. The logs dropped at his feet and he rushed forward. Her shoulders were slumped, head hanging low.

"Connin?"

His friend smiled. "Tio, smells like a good hunt, brother."

"Tiobald?" Her head came up and she looked around hopefully.

"Is everything to right? Did anything happen?" Tio asked of both Connin and Esmeralda.

"Completely uneventful. A little slow mayhaps, but—"

"Esmeralda?"

A slim smile pushed to her lips as her shoulders straightened. "I'm just tired."

He reached for her. After a moment's hesitation, she leaned down placing her hands on his shoulders. Her legs would not hold her and she clung to him.

He supported her and raised her chin with a finger. "What troubles you, Esmeralda?"

"Nothing."

"Please."

She shook her head free and dropped her gaze. "I'm glad to see you."

"You didn't believe I would be here? I told you where I went today."

"Yes, I know."

Again, he raised her chin. "Esmeralda, what troubles you? Speak of it so I may make it right."

She shook her head. But he wouldn't release her. Her words were whispered, and tears pooled in her gorgeous eyes. "You seemed… unsure. I feared you wished you'd chosen differently."

He drew her close, cradled her to his chest and kissed the top of her head. She was stiff at first, but she soon melted into his embrace. He'd meant to protect her, but he'd only stirred her fear and doubt. "Nothing could be further from the truth, Esmeralda. I couldn't have chosen a finer woman."

She looked up searching his face.

He smiled and stroked her back. "Come, let's get you something to eat. God blessed my hunt. He has provided well."

"Can… can we walk for a bit first."

Tio offered his arm with a chuckle. "A bit saddle sore?"

"Oh, beyond sore." She waddled in order to work the strain out her legs.

"Do you have anything in your bag that could help?"

"I do. I'll make a soothing tea with a touch of cloves for the pain."

Esmeralda barely ate as she watched him, then curled on her bedroll near the fire and was asleep almost instantly. His distance had backfired. But what would loving her cost them both?

Chapter 9

"Good morn, Wife."

"Good morn, Tiobald."

He tried not to show his disappointment at not being called husband again. "Did you sleep well?"

She smiled and nodded. But it wasn't true.

"Your sleep seemed troubled," he said searching her face.

She stopped folding her blanket and looked at him. "I thought you only watched me sleep the one night."

"I did not stay up all night, but anytime I woke, I saw you tossing about."

One shoulder rose and fell, as she returned her attention to the blanket. "I'm sure 'tis nothing to be concerned about."

But he was concerned. He needed to mend whatever he had broken —and quickly. He had the majority of the day before they arrived in Rustshade. It would have to be enough.

Yesterday, she had ridden all alone in a sea of warriors four men deep on any side. Today Tiobald rode beside her and their escorts were far removed by over three horse links.

"Why do they ride so far away?"

"To give us privacy."

Esmeralda looked him. Why did they need privacy? What was he going to tell her? Did he indeed change his mind and now planned to leave her somewhere? Did he intend to put her off quietly, as was the phrase?

"What is said between a husband and wife, no one else need be privy to," he smiled.

He confused her. From her experience, people either liked her or they didn't. His kiss had led her to believe one thing, but he had withdrawn since. Held her at arm's length almost. How did he feel?

"What are you thinking about when your gaze searches me so?" His smile was easy, and his ride relaxed.

"Tell me of your family." She turned back toward the road scanning the nearby foliage for anything she might want to use.

His voice was heavy. "I was one of the last males born in Rustshade. My older sister the last female. Mother died when she tried to bring forth a third child. Both died. Father did his best to raise us, but as more and more of the women died, he became morose. My sister died with her first child. Father, thought we should leave Rustshade and become part of other communities around us. But the elders at the time feared we would only bring our curse on them. Father died… a score ago now."

"My father too." She looked at him for a moment. "So, we are both orphans."

"I never thought about it much. Everyone in Rustshade has lost most of their family. I didn't see my situation as any different from them." He remained quiet for a short time. "What of your mother?"

"She died of a fever when I was but four summers."

"Who took care of you after your father died?"

"MeeMa."

He looked at her with a brow perched high.

"Old Widow Mia. Apparently as a child, I misspoke M-ia and said Mee-Ma and that is what I have always called her. She is a dear woman who taught me herbs and treatments, but the ignorant town branded her a witch. And me along with her."

A splash of color caught her eye. "Might we stop for a moment?"

"Do you require a rest?"

"No." She pointed to a clump of pale purple flowers. But looking back at him and pushed a smile to her lips. "Well, I would love to be out of this saddle. But that is saffron. It is good in warding off the rot."

"Connin." Tiobald yelled to one of the men at the front. "Hold."

The procession stopped and Tiobald was beside her horse before she could blink. She let him lower her but did not cling to him. Moving off to the plants, she carefully collected what she thought she could use.

When she stood and turned, she nearly ran into him. He lifted her chin. She was not accustomed to continually looking up at anyone. Few in Flatwell shared her height.

"Esmeralda, you spoke yesterday that you feared I regretted my choice. Do you regret your agreement?" Was that hurt in his steely gaze?

She snorted a bitter laugh and brushed passed him. "Heavens no. The tanner threatened to burn me at a stake if I wasn't chosen in the Culling. You saved my life."

He snatched her arm and spun her around. His other hand clenched tight. "They were going to kill you?" His voice was louder than she liked. She looked to see who else had heard him, but everyone seemed occupied in their own conversations.

"Aye. I told you that they thought me a witch."

"What made the tanner threaten you?"

Was he angry? With her? Or the tanner? "His babe was disquieted. Fussy. She had worn herself—and her poor mum—to exhaustion. I brought some soothing herbs. I put them in her basket to quiet her and gave others to her mum to make a tea. When the babe suckled, she would be soothed then as well."

"And for this, the tanner wanted to burn you alive? There was nothing else?"

"T'was all that was required. My people believe in old wives' remedies and are highly suspicious of anything else. They can't fathom how the Good Lord provided all manner of plants to aid in our health." She tried to pull free, but he held her still.

"What did you call your selection?"

"The Culling. What do you call it?"

"The Blessed Choosing."

"Well, I suppose it is a matter of perspective. Are you the one gaining a wife or the one losing your home and family?"

Only a sliver of air separated their bodies. He released her. "What do *you* call it?"

Locked in his gaze, his warm breath caressing her face, she wanted to throw her arms around his neck, pull him down, and let his lips claim hers again. But she couldn't move. His finger traced up her arm from the cuff, to the collar of her dress, to the bare skin of her neck. She quaked. His thumb stroked her jaw and brushed her lower lip, and her eyes closed. She wet her lips begging to be kissed.

"What do *you* call your selection, Esmeralda?" His lips were close to hers. They vibrated and warmed with his words. If she pushed up on her toes just a little…

She opened her eyes when they didn't connect. His gray eyes gleamed with mischief. He knew what she wanted but refused her. "Are you blessed or cursed?"

She slipped back on her heels and leaned away from him. "A little of both it would seem. You saved my life, Tiobald, but you seem bent on confounding me." She turned back to her horse and reached up to mount.

Tiobald seized her by the waist and nipped at her ear. "Then we are equally blessed and confounded."

She tried to jerk around. "How have I—" But he hoisted her up in the saddle with such speed, it took all her concentration not to go tumbling down the other side.

"Connin, proceed." He shot her a cheeky grin, and they began moving once more. He glanced at the sky. "Another couple of hours and we should be celebrating in Rustshade."

Esmeralda couldn't respond. Her thoughts and emotions were jumbled so thoroughly, she couldn't form a coherent thought. Like a spindle carelessly loosed from its wheel to tumble and unwind about the floor, she unraveled. And no matter what had happened to her, Esmeralda was never one to be out of sorts—not until she met tall, brooding, and confusing. She shot him a glance, and he still wore the smug smirk.

Whatever this game was, she didn't like it.

Chapter 10

An hour later, they turned off the road and entered a dense forest and Esmeralda lost sight of many of the men accompanying them. Twigs snapped and bits of conversation fluttered around the mighty trunks surrounding them. She shivered.

In the same moment she saw Tiobald's horse directly beside her, something flew over her shoulders.

"Not much sun breaks through until we get to Rustshade. There we have cleared the forest for our homes."

She pulled his heavy wool cloak tighter about her. "Thank you."

His knee brushed hers as the horses skirted between two slender trees. "I will always provide and protect you, Esmeralda." The conviction in his tone rattled her ribs.

"I never doubted."

"You seem unsure."

"No more than you, it would appear."

"I heard you well. You and your people saw our coming as a terror. Stolen—never to return—I think you said."

She nodded. "In truth, many think our women have been offered in some hideous sacrifice to a pagan deity. Or used for… sport."

"Well as I am the last to come for the Blessed Choosing, your people have nothing more to fear."

"The last? What of all these men with you? Do their wives still live?"

"Nay. Only four women remain. Their husbands stayed behind with the old men. Two are with child. We pray for their survival hourly."

"So, the men here?"

"They chose a wife and lost her. Their heartbreak will not allow them to choose again."

Esmeralda rubbed her arms at a chill not from the air. "It is a terrible burden to live one's life alone. No one to care for and no one to care."

"It is a worse trial to be impotent as you watch someone you love die."

She looked at him for several moments, but he did not return her gaze. "Is this why you hold me at a distance?"

His smirk returned. "I shall hold you as close as you like."

"Well you haven't so far," she muttered.

Trumpets sounded as they came over a rise. The leaves filled with the brassy call. Faint cheers were added to the horns. The forest area thinned as a palisade distinguished itself from the trunks of the living trees. Over four men tall, and sharpened to deadly points, it formed an undulating circle around wisps of smoke.

"Rustshade. Welcome."

In a spot of sunlight, the gates stood open wide. Wood-framed homes with plaster walls and thatched roofs clustered inside. Men lined a procession that Tiobald led her through. Cheers, waves, shouts of "Huzzah" and more trumpet calls marked her passing. This was far more than Flatwell ever did for their returning heroes.

As Tiobald helped her from the saddle one last time, outside what looked like a stable, she whispered. "Why are they so excited?"

"Every life is a joy. A blessing from the Most High. A chance for the curse to be lifted and a long future."

"I will do what I can to treat your women and children so they don't die." She worried her lower lip.

He spun her in his arms and rested his hands on her shoulders.

Warm and possessive. His words were quiet at first. "I pray your knowledge may indeed be the miracle we have been praying for, but it is not your burden to bear." When the last of the men who had traveled with them were inside the wall, and the gates shut, his words called out for all to hear. "Brothers, God has chosen the last of the women who may ever enter these gates. Esmeralda. And we pray for her good heath, long life, and healthy children." He pushed on her shoulders and whispered, "Kneel."

She sank to the ground as the entire town surrounded her sending a torrent of hummingbirds to take flight in her middle. Her breaths increased only to strangle in her throat when as many as could reach her laid their hands on her head and shoulders.

"Lord God, protect Esmeralda."

"Give her strength."

"Show her Your favor."

"Bless Tio and Esmeralda with a strong healthy family."

The prayers continued faster than a quiver of arrows could be loosed. A strange tingling—a presence—a strength—or mayhaps it was hope, danced over her skin leaving her awed and giddy.

"Lord, my Savior, I believe You have led me to the one You destined to be at my side. Help me to be a good husband. Give me strength to love her always, provide all she needs from Your hand, and protect her against all evil. May she only know love and peace. Thank You for Esmeralda, Father."

"Amen!" The men shouted as one, shaking the earth below her.

Before she could fully get up, Tiobald lifted her and cradled her in his arms. "To the feast. I want to dance with my bride."

Her heart now lodged in her throat. *Oh, Lord, help.* She never learned a single dance. Why would she? Who would court a witch?

Chapter 11

A long board laden with food sat raised on one side of an open area that was itself surrounded by more trestle tables and benches. The open-air gathering place seemed to be in the center of town. Shops, in the same fashion as the homes, lined the cobble streets beyond the tables, benches, and gathered men. From what Esz could see, there was no building large enough to house all of them for a celebration, so they ate here in the open with a flat patch of earth ringed by the tables—presumably for the dancing yet to come. Esz remained fixated on the spot sweat collecting in her palms.

As Tiobald released her, she looked down from the dais they shared with one other man. A sea of men stared back at her. Not another woman in sight. She inched closer to Tiobald, praying he did intend to protect her.

He leaned down and whispered in her ear. "You are the first new face in two summers. And the last who will be selected. They honor you. Do not fear."

Was she so easy to read?

"Welcome, Lady Esmeralda." The man sharing the place of honor bowed. "God's blessing be upon you." The man was much older then her husband; thinning gray hair peppered with dark strands was cut close to his scalp. His full face held a respectable number of wrinkles and kind eyes. He waved to a chair in front of her and Tiobald drew it out.

"This is Dunlang, our chief," Tiobald said taking the seat on her right placing her between the two men.

"Thank you, sir."

Dunlang patted her hand. "It is us who should be thanking you." He smiled. "God will bless us again. I feel it in my bones."

Tiobald squeezed her other hand calling out to the men milling about. "Are we feasting or clucking about like a gaggle of gossiping women?"

Men bowed; others hoisted tankers, "Aye, m'lord." Her cup was filled and she reached for it with a trembling hand. She didn't favor being made a spectacle. Too many bad things happened when she held the center of attention.

The cup contained an unusually flavored sweet mead. It frolicked across her tongue and splashed in her empty belly like a majestic waterfall into a pristine pool.

"You like it?" Tiobald said. "'Tis made from cenderberries, a local fruit in this area."

She only nodded as she took another drink.

While the revelry of the celebration swirled around them and grew, men who hadn't traveled with them came to Tiobald's side and whispered in his ear. To some, he nodded. Others, he scowled with a sharp incline of his head. What was so important that it needed to be attended to at this moment? Esz watched trying to decipher what was going on.

The assortment of meats, breads, and cheeses made her dizzy. As the men finished and took up their instruments, she bit into one speckled wedge of cheese and forced herself not to spit it out again.

Dunlang laughed. "'Tis a special variety only made here. From our other women and our rare visitors, I understand it is an acquired taste."

Esmeralda swallowed the mass in her mouth without further chewing and downed half her tankard of mead. Her stomach did somersaults, and her head swam with a low buzz. She stared at the foul concoction on her trencher and made mental note of its appearance so she might avoid ever tasting it again. A tremor raced through her entire body as she belched up a noxious aftertaste.

The music struck a note and Tiobald offered his hand. "Dance with me, Esmeralda." His smile was broad and inviting.

"I don't know how," she whispered and lowered her head. She didn't think the silly spins she did in the tavern were real dancing. She and Neal had only fluttered about.

"Trust me." He took her hand anyway and pulled her to the center of their gathering.

She bit her lip and fought for an even breath.

A man approached, whispered something to him, and disappeared. Tiobald eyes closed, and he frowned for a moment. Mayhaps she would be spared this humiliation.

But he looked at her with a sad smile and took hold of her forearms. The music set a rhythm and he tipped his head to his right. "Skip two steps." She followed awkwardly. "Back two." She did with little better results. "Two around." She didn't skip at all misunderstanding what he meant by around. She stumbled to keep her feet under her as they turned in a circle until she stood where he had moments ago. Barely gaining her equilibrium, he tipped his head to the side. "Again."

Two to the right. Two to the left. Switch. But this time when they turned around, he released her and Dunlang snatched her arms before she could fall backwards and land on her bum. They completed a circuit and she was passed off to the man called Connin.

In one spin, she caught a glimpse of Tiobald in another private conversation. She didn't have time to consider it as she was spun around again. She lost her footing when Connin released her to the next man. She fell back and slammed into Tiobald's arms.

They encircled her. "Take it easy on my bride, men. I will have need of her later."

The men laughed and heat crawled up her neck and filled her face. She tipped back her head and glared up at his rakish smile. She opened her mouth to respond and tried to gather her feet back under her, but a pain-filled shriek from one of the homes tore through the gathering.

Esmeralda jerked free of Tiobald.

The scream came again, and the men sobered. The music died. Everyone stilled.

She looked up at him for an answer.

He didn't look at her but in the direction of the cries. His voice was mournful. "Kel labors. The child again comes too soon. They are dying."

She tuned in the direction of the screams. "Take me to her."

He shook his head. "This is the way of things, Esmeralda. This is what I warned you about."

"And I may know how to save them."

For the first time in several moments, he looked at her. One brow arched high.

"What could it hurt? It is not as if I could make them any deader. Let me try."

His eyes searched her.

She started walking. "I'll find her myself."

Tiobald was beside her with the next step. "Are you sure?"

"I would never forgive myself if I danced the night away when I could have done something."

He led her to a home two lanes back from the town center and pushed open the door, but didn't follow. Lamps, hung from the ceiling and sat on tables, bathed the cramped space in glaring light. An agonizing screech came from an open door in front of her. Inside, two women talked gently to the woman lying in the bed drenched in sweat. They wiped her face with damp cloths. Mayhaps it was the light, or the palpable concern in the room, but all three women had an odd pallor about them. She would worry about that later.

"How can I help?"

The pregnant woman writhed as another pain overcame her.

The two tending her looked up. She didn't know any of these women. It appeared Rustshade culled—or chose—from more than just her town. The brunette spoke words of defeat. "She delivers too soon. The babe has not turned and she can't bring the child forth this way. It will be over soon."

"I can save them." The jolt ran through her at knowing why Peter's goat had labored at the very moment she walked by. It was so she might learn what she would now need. The knowledge made her entire body hum.

"What?" the other mousey-haired woman said.

"No, you don't understand. Nothing can be done—" the brunette said.

Esmeralda burst with excitement. "Truly. I know how to save—"

"You!"

Esmeralda turned at the angry bark coming from a raven-haired woman whose heart was even blacker than her locks. The last taken from Flatwell before her stood to her right. When she entered, she hadn't seen the woman. Esmeralda backed away from her hard glare and wagging finger.

"They chose *you*?" She turned to the other women. "Don't let Esmeralda touch Kel. She's a witch. She'll kill her for sure."

"Olva, I'm not—"

"Witch!" she bellowed.

"Olva!" The voice was Tiobald's. Esmeralda had not heard anyone so angry before now.

Chapter 12

Her raven-haired accuser flinched as if she'd been struck. Her head bowed. "Yes, m'lord."

"Shut your mouth, woman, and get out here."

"Yes, m'lord." Olva skirted Esmeralda with a sharp glare as she passed through the main room to the open door where Tiobald waited.

Tiobald's words were cutting and filled with rage. "That is my wife you accuse with your wicked tongue."

"But she—" Olva began to protest.

Through the open door, Esmeralda caught the swish of a mighty arm as Olva cowered almost to her knees. No contact was made, but the hand remained ready to strike.

"Only because you are with child, do I stay my hand. Get back to your home. If I hear a single whisper of your malicious slandering of the woman I have chosen—so help me, child or no, you will suffer a just punishment."

"Yes, m'lord." Olva scurried into the night.

Esmeralda came to stand beside him. He stared after Olva, his fists clenching and unclenching at his sides. After a moment, he asked in a raspy voice. "Can you do as you promised? Can you save them?"

"I believe so, if Kel has not labored too long. But surely they will not allow me to do what I must now with this taint on my name."

"Do it."

"But what of—"

"Will you stand and do nothing out of fear of what others say? Or will you do the thing you have promised?"

"I will do it if her husband agrees."

Tiobald scowled.

"To do what I must without his consent would only make Olva's words a permanent stain should it not be successful."

He waved over a man standing nearby. "Fetch Wilm. Tell him there may be hope, but he must hurry."

The man ran off in the opposite direction of the celebration. Esmeralda considered Tiobald as he continued. "Wilm prays in the chapel."

"Something we should all be doing, I suppose."

They waited, listening to Kel's intermittent screams. The mother's pains were not too close yet. There was still hope. Tiobald continued to clench and unclench his fists.

"M'lord?" she whispered.

He looked at her and blinked as if he had forgotten she stood beside him. "I am Second to Dunlang. I will be chief after him. Now I enforce the laws of the council and see punishments are carried out."

"A sheriff."

His brows drew together.

"It is the word we use for the man who assures the king's laws are followed."

"Sherriff." He tried the word and nodded as the first man returned with another. The new man wasn't much taller than she.

"There is hope?" the new man asked with skepticism.

"This is my chosen—Esmeralda. She thinks there is a way, but would not begin without your consent."

Another scream caused the man to cringe. "I want her saved. Both her and the child, if the Lord wills it. Do whatever you think will help."

She turned to Tiobald. "I need a knife, the sharpest you have."

Both men stared at her, jaws slacking.

"I also require a needle and stout thread and my satchel." She put her hand out. It took a moment for Tiobald to move, but he drew a short blade from his belt. Turning back to the door she said, "Stay close, both of you. I may need your assistance."

Tiobald barked orders to the man who had retrieved Wilm.

She put the blade in the hottest coals and came to Kel's side. "Hello, Kel." Esmeralda brushed her hand across the other woman's face. "I am Esmeralda. Wilm and Tiobald have agreed to let me help you. I know of a way that, Lord willing, will save both you and your babe. I have done it before with success." Well, she had helped anyway. "It will not be pleasant, but…"

"I don't wanna die." Kel pleaded as another pain overtook her.

"Esmeralda, your supplies," Tiobald called.

Turning to the brunette, she said, "Will you fetch those?" Esmeralda waved over the third women, the one with mousey hair, who bit at her fingers. "What's your name?"

"Jeni."

"Jeni, help me." They pulled the covers off Kel and pulled up her chemise until her writhing belly was laid bare.

The brunette handed her the items. Esmeralda set the thread and needle aside and dug through her herbs pulling out several. After she mixed them into a cup with boiling water from the fire, she lifted Kel's head. "This will help with the pain and soothe some." When Kel had finished, she placed a stick between the mother's teeth. "A few moments and the worst should be over."

Kel nodded.

"Jeni, hold her arms and shoulders still." She turned to the brunette.

"Heart."

Esmeralda stared at her.

"My name is Heart."

"Heart, hold her feet." The women took their places and Esmeralda drew the white-hot knife from the fire.

She paused and closed her eyes. "Lord God, guide my hand, and save Your precious children."

"Amen," Jeni and Heart whispered.

She felt for the babe and drew the knife over Kel's flesh. The woman screamed around the wood in her mouth. The first cut broke the skin but was not deep enough. More pressure. She made another cut perpendicular to the first forming an upside-down T on her abdomen. A few more draws of the knife along both cuts and she saw the babe. Pulling it from the mother, Esmeralda removed the sack and cradled him in her arm. He did not breathe. She placed her mouth over his nose and mouth and sucked gently. She'd seen MeeMa do it many times. She spit on the floor. It was as disgusting as she'd always imagined.

Nothing. "Oh, come, love," Esmeralda whispered. She tried to suck the material from his mouth once more as he turned a sickening shade of blue. Then she blew a small breath. Tapping and rubbing his chest, she blew again. No one else in the room made a sound. "Lord, please."

One more breath and the babe inhaled on his own and whimpered weakly.

The air was sucked from the room in a collective gasp.

"Tiobald, I need the smallest earthenware bowl you can find, no larger than your fist with a hole in the bottom," she shouted handing the babe to Heart.

"Aye."

"Wash him gently and quickly."

She turned back to the mother who managed a slim smile. "Almost over."

"Boy?"

"Yes. Kel. You have a son." She pulled the edges of the woman's skin together, then smeared the gaping wound with an ointment to ward off infection and started the stitches tight and neat. She was about half way done when she looked up to see if the women were done.

"Stop!" Everyone jumped. Esmeralda ran across space and snatched the lad from the women. "What in heaven's name are you doing?"

"We must rub him with salt to protect him from demons."

"Of all the fool-headed notions. That the good Lord is not powerful enough to protect an innocent from the wrath of hell … he is barely drawing breath, and you want to pickle him?" She dunked the lad up to his chin in the warm water to free him of the deadly substance. Repeating it until she was satisfied no salt remained.

She whirled on her heel and entered the main room. "Wilm, I need you."

He stepped in the home, Tiobald had to duck as he entered behind him with the bowl.

"Remove your tunic."

"What?" both men nearly shouted in the same instant.

"Goose feathers to the highest heavens, I did not ask the man to undress. I need to place your son against your skin. You must share your heat with him, and you can't do that with your shirt on."

After Tiobald nodded his consent, Wilm stripped to the waist.

"Sit," she inclined her head to a chair near the hearth of the fire shared by both rooms. She laid the babe, chest to chest with his father, and placed Wilm's hands so they covered and supported the fragile baby. Glancing around the room she pointed. "Tiobald, the blanket."

He brought it, and she wrapped it around both father and son covering all but the babe's face. She took the bowl he also handed her, placed it over the baby's face and helped the dad hold it steady as he cradled his son.

She snatched up the bellow and showed Tiobald how to blow air through the hole in the bottom. "Tiny, slow, easy puffs." Turning to the father she said. "Talk to him or hum. The vibrations of your voice will help keep him connected here. Your warmth, your strong heartbeat, and your voice will remind him of growing in his mum."

He nodded and she returned to Kel. The poor woman was asleep. Esmeralda hoped the new mum was exhausted enough not to wake as she finished the remaining stitches.

She put another layer of the ointment on the incision and covered Kel, before returning to the men.

"Is she?" Wilm looked up searching her face.

"She still draws breath. Lord willing, they will both make it through the night. Each day will see them stronger and more likely to survive." She glanced around the room, then poked her head back into the sleep chamber. Heart and Jeni sat beside the bed watching over Kel.

Esmeralda spoke to them. "We will take shifts to watch over her. One of you can start and the other go home and rest. We will need you in the morning."

She came back to the men. "You are ill prepared for caring for a child."

"What do you lack?" Tiobald asked without looking up from his task.

"Nappies, swaddling blankets, a cradle will be needed."

"Newt?" Tiobald called over his shoulder never disturbing his consistent rhythm of air.

Her next order relayed to the man who had fetched Wilm, Esmeralda returned to Kel and mixed another tea for her pain. Heart remained. "When she wakes, pour hot water in this and have her drink it."

She took the boy from his father to apply a small nappy made from soft cloth she found before Newt returned. Without his father's warmth the babe squirmed and let out a cry. "Well my, don't you sound better. Keep crying, little one; will make your lungs stronger."

"Crying is good?" Wilm said.

"In this case, yes. Not for over long, but the more he uses his lungs, the stronger they will become and the better chance he will survive now and through the harsh winters to come."

With the baby covered so he wouldn't mess on his father, she returned him. "Let him go a bit without the air. Your heartbeat will comfort him like his mum's did. Your heat will ward off any chill. He will want to feed soon, but I don't want to wake his mum just yet. She needs her rest as much as he."

She straightened and stretched as she moved to the door. Outside, she leaned against the house and looked up at the stars twinkling between the trees. A sliver of moon cast the dirt lane in a gentle glow.

"You did it." Awe colored Tiobald's words and danced in his eyes.

"The Lord saw fit to save them."

"But He used you to do it."

She glanced down at her beautiful gown. "'Tis ruined."

"There are other dresses. 'Twas a price worth paying."

Her smile was washed away in a huge yawn.

He handed her a cup and she brought it to her lips. Bitterness washed over her tongue, thick with minerals. She spit it out. "What is this?"

"Water?"

She pushed off the wall. "Where does it come from?"

"The well?" Tiobald's brows were drawn together as he pointed.

"This is the water—" she looked to the house. "Oh good Lord, save us." She dropped the cup and bolted through the door.

"What's the matter?"

"The water is poison, and I just washed the babe in it."

Chapter 13

Esmeralda flew through the house dumping over pitchers, cups, and even the pot hanging over the fire. The flames sputtered as steam and disturbed ash sent the men to coughing. Esmeralda spun in frantic disjointed circles trying to make her weary brain think clearly.

"What are you doing?" Tiobald's fists clenched in rhythm again.

"Is there any fresh water? A stream or lake nearby?"

"There is a stream about a half an hour north of here."

"Send men. Fill as many containers as they can carry—"

Tiobald grabbed her by the shoulders and held her still. The warmth and firmness of his touch soothed and quieted her. "We all drink from the well. There is no poison. And it is the wee hours of the morning. Surely it can wait until first light."

"'Tis not a poison like a snake bite that kills immediately. What is in the well will cause a wasting disease. It weakens the body." She pointed at Wilm who stood cradling his son. "The babe is already weak from coming too early and a long labor. Do you say he can survive being bathed in a substance that will weaken him further?"

Tiobald's shoulders shagged, "Newt?"

She followed him outside a moment later.

"I also require balyum leaves." She showed Newt one. The thin man touched it, his shaggy hair covered his eyes. "As many as you can find."

When he raced off to wake others, she turned to Tiobald. "The beef we feasted on? When was it butchered?"

"Only a few hours before we arrived. Why?"

"If the hide is still in good condition, I need a teat. And I need fresh milk from a cow that has not recently drank from the well."

"But Kel?"

"Is full of the toxin from the tainted water. She can't nurse her son until she is free of it. The leaves will speed the process. A day, mayhaps two. But he is hungry now." The babe whimpered from inside the home as if to punctuate her point.

Newt returned just then, and Tiobald sent him off on his next tasks. "You should rest."

"When the babe is fed and Kel has begun her treatment."

Esmeralda poured the fresh cow's milk and a sprinkling of herbs in a jar little bigger than her hand. She secured the bit of cow udder on top with many loops of twine and took it to Wilm. "Turn him over so he lays in your arm, but keep his head up."

The baby squirmed and squeaked. She handed Wilm the jar. "Offer it to him." The babe didn't take to it right away. After several attempts, she squeezed the teat releasing a small stream into his mouth. He finally closed his mouth around it. After a time, he got the hang of it and drained the milk quickly. She showed Wilm how to pat his back removing the gas and she refilled the jar.

She had just handed it back to Wilm when the men returned with the fresh water. They had grumbled at first at having been woken in the middle of the night, but when they learned both Kel and the babe still lived, they sprang to the task and then returned to renew the celebration that had ended hours earlier.

Warming a bit of the fresh water, she washed the babe three times, hoping all the minerals from the well water were removed before returning the lad to his father. Both were asleep before she turned her attention to Kel. Soaking the balyum leaves in a special selection of her herbs. She woke Kel. "Sorry, my friend, but I need you to rise so I might prepare your bed. Be easy, and go slow." She helped Kel from bed rolling her to her side first.

Kel smiled, "I never thought to see this day. The day *after* I gave birth."

"You still have a lot of healing to do."

Kel nodded as Esmeralda and Heart helped her stand. They supported her over to the chamber pot. Then they had Wilm bring their son. Tears coursed down her face as she brushed her hand over what little of his face could be seen. "'Tis the most beautiful child."

Heart supported Kel while Esmeralda prepared her bed. She stripped the soiled sheet and replaced it with a clean one and a layer of soaked balyum leaves. When Heart brought Kel back, they removed her chemise and helped her lay down in a comfortable position before they covered her in another layer of leaves.

Esmeralda put a sheet over her and left Heart to keep watch. Tiobald waited near the door. The first rays of light were just lighting the sky.

"Now, you need to sleep." It was an order.

She inclined her head and made to follow him. "I need a sturdy wood chair with the seat removed."

Tiobald stopped and his brows drew tight together.

"To place over the chamber pot. Kel can't crouch with stitches in her gut."

He nodded.

"So, 'tis true?"

They both turned. Dunlang strolled up to them with a big smile. "They both live?"

"Aye, Esmeralda has done the impossible." Tiobald's shoulders pushed back and his chin rose.

"God saved them," she curtsied. Between the three-day horse ride and being on her feet much of the night, she was stiff—her muscles tender.

Dunlang bowed, "But He saved none until you came, m'lady." He turned to stroll away.

"Would you like to see him?" Esmeralda offered.

"We'll all meet him when the time is right. I'll see you at the council meeting later."

"She is tired and in much need of rest." Tiobald said.

"I would hear more of this concern over our well."

Tiobald's fists began clenching and unclenching as he led her back toward the hamlet square. "You will get at least a couple of hours sleep before everyone can wake and gather."

Chapter 14

Esmeralda's steps slowed, she swayed slightly.

Tio clenched his jaw and scooped her into his arms.

Her warm arms snaked around his neck, and she clung to him. Her head tucked under his chin. Her breath slipped under his tunic collar. She melted into him as if she were part of him. She was fast becoming so.

He picked up his speed as his body warmed to her nearness. The screams of a dying mother had reminded him of all the reasons he'd long refused to choose. Esmeralda could never be forced to endure such. Tio pushed open the door of his home—their home—and walked her to the sleeping chamber. He let her legs fall to the floor. She startled awake and looked around. Sure she wouldn't fall, he released her and stepped away. "Get some sleep." He reached to pull the door closed, but she came to him.

"You need sleep as well." It was an invitation. Offered in innocence, but filled with passion.

"You're too tired." He closed the door before the hurt in her eyes could trap him into staying. He busied himself stoking the fire to a bright crackling glow. Hoping it would burn away his feelings.

He sat staring at the flames. Every muscle ached. He let his eyes close and his head hang. His forearms rested on his thighs. Tio hadn't wanted to bring any women into this life. Love should not be offered, then stolen in a horrible death. The others had demanded it. He had been the last to give in. Esmeralda had been different than any they brought before—bold, strong, challenging him to choose her.

Their kiss. His tongue ran over his lips, tasting her again. Passion met him in that moment. A feeling he never wanted to find. He dared hope she would be strong enough to face a life with him. But when he learned of her losses, her mother and father dying when she was so young and the rejection of her town, it tore him. She was fragile in a way he could not imagine. He needed to keep her safe. Comfort her. But never get too close.

But mayhaps.

His fists clenched. He rolled his shoulders against the tightness boring deep inside.

Olva, that foul creature, had already maligned Esmeralda's name. The woman had been the worst choice of any of the men. Sharp tongued. Disagreeable. More than once she had suffered reprimand for her venomous words. Esmeralda had been in the shire but a few hours and already the stink of *witch* hung about her neck.

He'd spoken to Jeni when she'd left and was assured she would not repeat the moniker.

"Truly, m'lord, I witnessed no witchcraft. Your lady wife prayed. Pleaded with the Lord when the babe did not first draw breath. There were no spells cast and no potions. She employed nothing more than the healers and midwives of my own home. Though I feared greatly when she cut the babe from my dear friend, it was a surgery as best I as have ever witnessed."

Though he was satisfied of Jeni's feelings concerning Esmeralda's work, he still needed to speak with Heart.

Esmeralda had clearly saved Kel and the babe with skill—not any dark magic. The first to survive in Rustshade in nearly three score of years. How many women had been sacrificed? How many babes never drew their first breath? Was the curse over? Was there hope for him and Esmeralda? Did he dare allow himself to love her?

His elbows dug into his knees as he gripped his aching head. Mayhaps, just mayhaps, there was hope. But he had to be sure. For in truth, he already loved Esmeralda. And he would not sacrifice her.

A bubble of laughter escaped his lips. Seeing Wilm act nursemaid. She had called him, a brazen thing for a woman to do, and asked him to undress—well remove his tunic. But the babe's survival had been her only concern. She'd placed the small life in the warrior's mighty hands. She never noticed his discomfort as she directed him. Tio's smirk grew. Of all the men in the shire to care for such a fragile life, Wilm would have been the last choice. But he had done well.

Would he one day hold his own son cradled do his chest? Esmeralda's son?

Lord, please let the curse be over.

Chapter 15

The sound of fluttering fabric filled the room. The fire was little more than embers. He turned to see Esmeralda in the deep blue gown he had left for her. A long slit opened down the back of each sleeve. Intervals of ribbons bound it closed leaving only four oval openings for the stark white of her underdress to peek through. Some of the ribbons dangled untied.

She ran her hand over the skirt drawing his eye to the belt accentuating her narrow waist. She smiled. "'Tis ever so beautiful, but I fear ruining the fine velvet." She raised her arm with a wiggle to send the long tail of the sleeve end to swinging. "These will be especially hard to keep clean."

Tio stood in awe and stared at her. Words wouldn't form as all but her beauty was driven from his mind.

"Mayhaps the tanner could make an apron for me?"

He nodded.

She came toward him. Her smile tentative.

Alertness fired in his brain like an arrow whizzed past his head. He jerked. His body became straight and his skin hummed. "Break the fast?" The words choked in his throat and his voice cracked. He cleared it giving a slight shake to his head in a desperate attempt to break free. "Come, eat something."

The smile faded and she turned to the door. "I couldn't keep food down. Not with the meeting before the council looming before me."

"Esmeralda …" She was already out the door.

She stood in the bright sunlight shading her eyes. "Good morn to you, Newt."

"Good morn, m'lady."

She took a few tentative steps forward. "Now, you didn't remain outside while we slept?"

"No," he chuckled. "I just arrived. The council is gathering."

A shudder twitched across her shoulders as Tio came up behind her.

"I'll check on Kel and her babe first."

"Esmeralda, the council—" Tio tried to steer her to the meeting room.

"Will wish to know the current standing of the patients. Now…" She turned and took a faltering step clearly unsure of which way to go.

"This way, m'lady," Newt offered before Tio could direct her otherwise.

She walked beside Newt though the young man tried to let her precede him as protocol dictated. He cast a nervous glance over his shoulder. Tio nodded to reassure him he saw what Newt tried to do.

"Now, Newt, if it is not too bold of me, may I ask, you seem younger than the other men. Tiobald spoke of his birth as the last in Rustshade."

"I was not born here, m'lady." Another glance over his shoulder came accompanied with a smile. "M'lord came to a choosing in my home of Silver Bend. He was one of the men to search the town. I was an orphan on the street and followed him through the town and out the gate. At the end of the first day, he made a place for me by the fire, and I rode on his horse the rest of the way to Rustshade. I have served as his squire ever since, too grateful to do anything else."

She nodded. "A appreciative heart is a powerful thing to be sure."

Newt stopped at the door of Wilm's home with a bow. She knocked softly and poked her head in before disappearing inside. She was a bold thing.

"Newt, would you be a dear and collect some more milk, please?" she called from within.

"Of course, m'lady."

Esmeralda had changed the babe's nappy by the time Tio entered. Wilm wore dark circles below his eyes. "Didn't sleep well?" Tio patted him on the shoulder.

"Each time I drifted off he'd wiggle or squeak. I feared I didn't hold him tight enough or too tight. Twice I almost fell from the chair and scared us both." The tension in Wilm's voice matched Tio's own.

"Well, he has come through the worst of it. Looks alert and hale." Esmeralda reached for a blanket and wrapped him tight. She handed him to Tio who tried to refuse the babe. "I need one of you to move the cradle into the bedchamber, and the other to hold the boy. If you would rather the cradle…" She moved to hand the boy to his da.

Tio thrust out his arms and she wrapped them around the boy till the lad was safely tucked in the crook of his arm.

Wilm moved the cradle and Esmeralda retrieved the milk from Newt at the door. Tio was sure he didn't breathe.

"Put the babe's bed beside his mum."

Wilm returned a moment later as she finished securing the teat on the jar again. She held out the container as Tio passed the lad to his da. "Feed him while I check Kel and change the balyum leaves. Then you can place him in the cradle and you can rest with your wife."

"The council—"

"Can wait a handful of moments more."

Obstinate. The woman had yet to do what he asked.

She seemed to be inside the bedchamber forever. When at last she emerged all the ribbons on her sleeves were tied. She nodded to Wilm who handed her the empty jar. "The leaves did well. I will check on her after the council." Her words shook. Did she fear what would happen in the meeting? "Pat him before you lay him down. Then all of you get some sleep."

She stepped from the home, stopped, and took a deep breath. She unwound the sleeve ends she had tucked out of the way, brushed her hands over her gown, and touched her plaited and wound hair. One more deep breath and she squared her shoulders.

"Okay, I am as ready as one can be to stand before the town council of a foreign shire." Fear flavored each word.

Tio should have taken her hand. Hugged her. Or at least offered her words of comfort. He had none. Never had one of the wives been summoned. Well, other than Olva to face reprimand, but even that didn't come in the first year. Esmeralda hadn't even been here a full day.

Lord, help them.

Chapter 16

They entered a common room with a raised dais at the front. Dunlang sat on it behind the table and a chair remained empty beside him. Talking amongst themselves, eight men sat behind two more long boards extended along each wall facing the center.

"Wait here until you are called," Tiobald whispered in her ear. He and Newt continued past her. Tiobald took the empty chair on the dais and Newt stood two steps behind his left elbow.

Dunlang said something calling the men to order. She could not catch the words as she fought to calm her frantic breathing. How far had Olva's hatefulness spread? Had she escaped one fire only to be tossed on another? Did any of it matter? Kel and the babe were alive, *Thank you, Lord.* But she feared her husband regretted his choice. He pulled from her touch. Mayhaps he also believed her a witch.

"Lady Esmeralda?"

She blinked. Had they called her and she missed it? Tiobald's gazed was narrowed as he looked at her. She stepped forward and curtsied to the floor. She moved further into the room. Her legs quaked beneath her. Two steps. Three. One more and she stood in the place between to the side tables and directly in front of the dais. "M'lords." She gave another deep observance.

"We welcome you with great joy to our shire, m'lady." Dunlang's voice was strong but gentle. "Would you tell us of Kel and her babe?"

"Both are doing well. The babe has eaten a few times. Kel has been up and walked about with minimal assistance."

The buzz of a thousand bees filled the room as the men discussed her information.

Tiobald put his fingers in his mouth and gave a sharp whistle. The room came to order once more.

Dunlang inclined his head. "'Tis a miracle, m'lady."

"We serve a mighty God." She bowed her head.

A smattering of "amen's" encircled her.

Dunlang rested his arms on the table. "Can you tell us of your concerns about the water we draw from our well?"

She drew in a slow breath and released it. "M'lords, I can show you the taint in the water. If I may?"

Dunlang looked to Tiobald and they both nodded.

She directed her words to Newt. "I will need two basins with water. One from the well and one from what was brought from the stream. Do not tell me which is which."

Newt nodded and darted from the room.

She again addressed Dunlang. "There are unseen particles, or minerals, in the well water, which are causing the premature births in your women. As the mum consumes the water, these hidden bits can cause the babe to arrive too soon. Neither are then strong enough to survive."

"How can this be if we all drink from the same water, eat the same food prepared with it, and all bathe in it?"

"If I might be so bold, m'lord. Do the men ever leave the palisade other than choosing your wives?"

"The men hunt." Tiobald said. "We leave every couple of days in one or two groups to collect the food for our meals."

"And do the men take water from the well in skins? Or do they drink from the surrounding springs?"

"Springs," Dunlang and Tiobald said as one.

The buzz began again.

"We did not drink water from your well on my journey here."

Tiobald shook his head.

"But the women *only* drink of the well." Dunlang leaned back in his chair and stroked his chin.

The hum in the room was almost hard to speak over. "Yes, m'lord. Their continued exposure, and the fragile nature of the wee babes, made them more vulnerable to the effects of the minerals."

Newt returned with the items she requested. "Place the basins on the table before the lords." She slipped her hands behind her back and clasped them tightly together. "Again, do not indicate which contains the well water and which the fresh, but be sure you know which is which."

Newt inclined his head.

She pulled the satchel over her head and handed Newt also. "Dump out the contents on that table." She indicated a square table beside her with a raise of her chin.

"Take the yellow pouch, the one with a red cord—"

"Would it not be easier if you did it?" Tiobald tipped his head.

"I will not. I want no one to say I tainted the test. If my hands touch none of the ingredients, and I do not know which basin contains the foul water, then I cannot be accused of bending the results to my will. The outcome will be fact and not something of my own conjuring."

Mumbled agreement floated about the room as she directed Newt to two other pouches and the mortar and pestle. The remaining contents were returned to the satchel and it was set aside.

In a few moments, the ingredients were ground to her exacting instructions. Newt carried the mortar to Tiobald and Esmeralda turned her back to the basins. "Take an equal pinch, drop it into each container of water and stir."

A gasp was followed by scrapping chairs as the men to her right and left stood to look in the water.

Esmeralda turned slowly, though none but Tiobald looked at her. "The black water is from the well."

"Aye, the water in the left basin is from the well," Newt confirmed.

Clumped together near the dais, the men talked overtop each other until an ear-piercing whistle sent them back to their seats.

"Well, m'lady, you have certainly made an impression. We will discuss the best way to deal with the threat to our women and children." Dunlang offered a kind smile.

She curtsied. "If I have found any favor before you, might I address one other matter?"

Dunlang waved out his hand, "Proceed, m'lady."

From beside him, Tiobald frowned.

"With your livestock, how do you go about strengthening your animals?"

Again, the men on the high platform exchanged glances. Tiobald answered. "Horses we put in a corral and run on a lead. We will take them out on journeys. Each time increasing speed and distance." This last word was left with a question in the air.

Esmeralda continued. "And how do you break a volatile horse?"

"We hobble it," Dunlang said. "Put it inside a stall in the stable away from the other animals and only the owner has any contact with the creature."

"And what do you do to a woman who is found to be with child?"

"We send her abed." The whispered response came from her left. Other voices began interjecting.

"We are breaking our women."

"Weakening them."

"We do them a disservice."

The answers shot back and forth from the men on either side of her like volleys from enemy lines.

"We have heard you, Lady Esmeralda. Thank you for coming to

speak with us." Dunlang stood and bowed. "If you would be so kind as the leave us to our discussions?"

She curtsied, collected her satchel, and turned.

"Go rest," Tiobald said.

Newt joined her outside as she stood and breathed several slow deep breaths. "Let me show you the way home."

She pointed. He laughed and pointed in almost the opposite direction.

"I will get my bearings soon, I hope." She shrugged. "Might I see Kel before I return?"

He bowed and led the way.

The treatment was working and Kel would soon be free enough of the toxins to nurse her babe. Soon Esmeralda stood alone in what was now her home. Somehow, being married to Tiobald had made her feel more alone than at any time in Flatwell. Tears burned her eyes. Was this luxurious, many-roomed home with a raised feather-mattress bed now her prison?

Chapter 17

Esmeralda surveyed Tiobald's home. The place she would live—until he asked her to leave. It seemed clear he didn't want her here. She stifled a sigh as she glanced about.

The main living area was larger than MeeMa's entire home. To the right stood a tall cutboard against the wall with a shelf of spices perched above it. A few bowls and trenchers were stacked on one end, and four pots of various sizes hung from the wall. Between the preparation area and the door sat a table with an odd assortment of four chairs. Some had arms and others cushioned seats.

Directly across from the door, the hearth shared its fire with the bedchamber. Three doors shared the inner wall with the hearth. Two were closed, while the door to the bedchamber she used last eve remained open.

She tossed a couple of pieces of wood in the hearth to keep the coals alive. Even in autumn, Rustshade's shadowed lands stayed warm enough that a full fire was not needed. But come evening, the coolness would require one. Better to keep the fire alive now than let the house become chilled later.

She glanced at the rather open space to her left. A narrow table sat under the window beside the door. An orderly stack of rolled parchments sat on one side of it.

Mayhaps she could string some rods from the ceiling for drying her herbs opposite the desk. She wondered if Tiobald would allow the scattered nature of herbs in various stages of drying to coexist in his well-ordered world.

She rubbed her arms and moved into the bedchamber. The large, raised feather bed piled high with coverings and pillows dominated the room. Her heart mourned for a simple hayloft and MeeMa to dote over her. She had left a challenging life and entered the pit of hell. Tiobald didn't favor her. He kept her at a distance. Even when he carried her to his home, his touch held no warmth. He couldn't get away from her fast enough as he dropped her feet on the floor and fled the room.

She climbed atop the covers and cried herself to sleep.

After adding two more branches on the fire, Esmeralda passed through the empty living area and stepped out into the filtered early afternoon light. The trees surrounding the shire were a palate of colors twinkling in the soft breeze. A walk would settle her spirit.

She entered the shire square to find the well destroyed. The walls encircling it were smashed and pushed in the opening. The wood roof lay splintered atop the broken stones. She smiled. Never again would anyone drink its tainted water.

She should check in on Kel and her babe.

"Lady Esmeralda?" Dunlang strolled toward her with quick purposeful strides.

She curtsied. "M'lord."

Tiobald hastened behind him a moment later.

"I am told you would not allow the women to protect the babe from evil?" His curt words mirrored his eye's intensity.

"'Tis true. A bath in salt would have burned his fragile skin and killed him, m'lord."

"But, m'lady, what of the child's immortal soul? Something must be done." He crossed his arms and his toe tapped.

Tiobald did nothing to assist her. The end of the union had come—already.

"As I told Jeni and Heart, m'lord. I believe we serve a mighty and most powerful God. One more than capable of shielding His precious children until such an age where they make their choice to follow the Lord or their own sinful desires."

Dunlang relaxed. "Surely, there is something we can do?"

"A priest or monk can dedicate the babe to the Lord as God's people have done for a thousand years."

"Remember the terseness of the monk who wed us in the wilderness? Holy men do not visit here. They believe Rustshade cursed. We count ourselves fortunate that they allow us to go to them for our marriages and last rites," Tiobald said.

"Well, that monk blessed us." *Not that it matters when your husband doesn't want you.*

Dunlang turned a quizzical look to Tiobald. "How'd you manage to get that sanctimonious nit to speak blessing over you?"

Her husband smiled—at her. "Esmeralda, insisted. Would not let the man be until he spoke the words."

"I would be more than willing to do so again. Must we ride two days to get to him?"

"Nay, there is another monk not far from here. He comes within sight of the shire walls to offer last rites, but no closer." Tiobald scowled.

Her fists perched on her hips. Tiobald's gaze followed their movement. A gentle color warmed his face. Was he still considering her?

She shook off the emotions warring within her and directed her words to Dunlang. "If you send Newt to call the monk forth immediately, I will do all in my power to bring the man here for the blessing." She pointed to the sealed well. "Clearly, the wise men of Rustshade have removed the ailment that led the holy men to foolishly believe you cursed."

Dunlang's head cocked to the side. "And you believe you can convince the monk to come?"

Tiobald stood tall, shoulders back, chin high. "If any can accomplish such a feat would be Esmeralda."

Mayhaps there was still hope for them.

Chapter 18

Esz failed to find a moment to talk with her confounding husband. He dashed off to instruct Newt to go to fetch the monk. Next, he managed to avoid her as he saw to saddling his horse and Esz's white mare himself. She was again left to her own as her husband avoided her. Back at Kel's home, after some coxing, they convinced her babe to nurse.

Esz stepped back into the height of the afternoon and wandered a bit. As she searched for the chapel, she bumped into a man and asked for directions. He bowed several times and glanced around as though he were a deer and wolves were howling. At last he pointed and dashed away.

The building sat east of the square near the palisade. Unremarkable, simple, and square, it held little more than scattered dust-covered pews and a table atop the dais. The aisle remained clean and worn due to visitors coming to seek petition before the cross hanging on the wall at the front of the building.

Esmeralda knelt and bowed her head. "Lord God, I believed You called me here. You have provided me with much learning and extensive practice that I might come and aid Your children. I dared hope I would find a home in this new town, Father. Help me endure. Give me strength and wisdom, and though Tiobald rejects me, help me to be kind.

"Grant me insight and bring to mind the instructions of the monks from my youth as I confront this ignorant holy man concerning Your divine leading. Fill my mouth with Your words and lead both the monk and me according to Your will."

She remained silent and still before the altar, hoping for… for anything. A thought, a verse, a touch, peace, strength. But as always, God remained silent for her. She never heard His gentle, quiet voice.

Still unsettled as she left the chapel, she wandered without thought until she nearly collided with Jeni coming around a home. The woman threw her arms around Esmeralda with a squeal. "They live. 'Tis ever so exciting." She took Esmeralda's hand and pulled her along. "The men can talk of nothing else. And…" she stopped, glanced about, and leaned close as she whispered with a giddy titter, "My Zeke has become ever so amorous." She covered her face with her hand as she laughed.

Jeni started pulling her along again. "Everything has changed. It reminds me of harsh winters from my home in the north. Endless dark days inside, buffeted and battered by the weather outside. Then one day, the sun reappears and life begins again."

Jeni led her to a garden tucked near the back of the palisade and finally released her. Well-tended vegetables grew in abundance even this late in the season. "This has been my contribution to my new home. I have been touched with a love for growing things. Now you bring a knowledge of healing." She sighed with satisfaction. "I can't wait to be with child. To someday share this with my daughter, oh, 'tis my only prayer." She bounced up as if a bee had stung her behind. "Oh, because of you, I truly can't wait to get with child now."

Esmeralda startled. "I pray all is as you say. One live babe does not mean all is righted."

"One babe. One mum. Fresh water. I feel better already. Everything has changed for the good I know it." Jeni threw her arms around Esmeralda's neck again. "Bless you, Esmeralda. The Lord bless you as you have blessed us."

Jeni's gratitude worked a balm into her battered spirit. She returned the woman's embrace as a weight lifted off her. They turned and discussed her garden. Esmeralda asked if she could plant some of her herb seeds on the far side.

Jeni squealed again and took both her hands. "'Tis why I brought you here. Give me whatever you wish grown and I will tend to it with much love."

"Thank you, Jeni. This garden will be most helpful."

As they ambled back to the shire center, Jeni listed which of Esmeralda's seeds could be planted now and which should wait till spring."

"Esmeralda!" Her peace shattered at Tiobald's bellow. His eyes locked with hers, but she couldn't read the emotion brewing in their silver depths.

Chapter 19

Esmeralda shrank from him as he stomped toward her. He hadn't been able to find her, and his heart had filled with such fear it nearly strangled him. Someone thought she went to see Kel, another to the chapel, and another that she had returned to their home.

Jeni propped a fist on one hip. "Do not scold your lady wife, m'lord. I took her to the garden, and we have made plans to grow her healing herbs."

He tried to force his heart out of his throat and to stop his fists from clenching and unclenching. Seeing Esmeralda, hale and smiling, had nearly sent him hurtling into her arms. "All fine and good, Jeni, but the monk awaits our arrival. Esmeralda, come."

She inclined her head and followed without a word. His abrasive words did nothing to calm her shudder or raise her downcast gaze. He knew she needed him to be soft, but such tenderness would endanger the distance he needed between them until he knew loving her would not kill her—and him in turn. He could not lose another he loved.

She mounted her horse without his help. He should have been grateful he didn't have to touch her in his current state, yet he resented that she didn't need him.

They rode the entire half hour in silence, her shoulders slumped. She dismounted on her own when they reached the two brown-robed men. A new slender, young monk stood beside Brother Sabistine, the gnarled senior monk.

"Where is your dead?" Sabistine's voice rasped and sent a shiver over his skin.

"There are no dead. But there is new life. A life requiring a blessing. You must come at once." Esmeralda ordered the pair with a wave of her hand to their donkeys.

"A child has been born in Rustshade?" Sabistine nearly choked on the words.

"Yes, a strong lad. They tried to bathe them in salt out of fear he would be taken by demons, because you will not bless them. Now come."

"It is forbidden to enter that cursed shire. A bit of salt on the tongue will ward off the evil."

Esmeralda stomped up to him and waved her finger at his nose. "Christ Himself said, 'Suffer little children, and forbid them not, to come unto me: for of such is the kingdom of heaven.' Do not come between the Lord God and this child or you, monk, will suffer the fires of hell." Her fists slammed onto her hips. "Tell me where it is written that the men of God should not go where God's people are? The shepherds are to lead the flock, yet you have abandoned them on a fool notion. Their water was poor. No more besets this shire. Yet you neglect God's people."

"But all the women who have come before have died. 'Tis a curse of God to cause so much death."

"You accuse Almighty God of evil?"

Sabistine sputtered, unable to reply. Newt gasped and shifted from foot to foot beside Tio.

"I contend that *if* God has withheld his blessing from Rustshade, 'tis because of *you*. 'Greet all the brethren with an holy kiss.' Yet you offer no kiss, nor greeting of any kind, only indifference to their needs. Our Lord Himself said, 'But I say unto you which hear, love your enemies, do good to them which hate you, Bless them that curse you, and pray for them which despitefully use you.' Not a man, woman, or child in Rustshade is your enemy. None have cursed or persecuted you. Do they not deserve more than an enemy? They have cried out for your aid and you have rebuffed them out of spite and fear. The Lord call you to account for your hatred." Her words did not threaten, her voice did not rise. It filled with a strength and conviction that made Tio quake. Newt and the young monk shuddered as well.

The woman was a force and the very hand of God.

"I will go with them," the young monk said in the quiet left after Esmeralda's words. He had stood silent, head bowed, fingers tracing the beads at his waist.

"Brother Joanis, you cannot visit that shire. Regardless of what this brazen woman says, I tell you there is evil within."

Joanis raised his head and smiled at Esmeralda. "Nay, Brother. Evil would not seek God's blessing. Satan would not invite the holy into his walls. And he would not send one so filled with my Lord's holy presence and speaking His sacred Words to come and drive out any evil that may perchance have dared enter into Rustshade. And nay, again Brother, I do not go merely to bless the child. I go to live amongst these people. God calls me to teach and love them, for *He* surely does."

Tio reeled from the shock.

Sabistine turned red. Spittle flew with his words. "Brother Joanis, I forbid you to abandon your appointment to—"

Joanis moved to his donkey's side and prepared to mount. "We know we not told, 'We ought to obey God rather than men.' God calls me to these people and I will obey my Lord."

"God deal with you, be it ever so harshly, for the sins you have committed against the good people of Rustshade, Sabistine," Esmeralda said as she mounted her horse.

"I am a Brother of the holy order of—"

"You are no brother of mine." She turned her horse and rode beside

Brother Joanis as Tio and Newt scrambled into their saddles.

"Your lady wife is touched of God, m'lord," Newt said.

"The woman could truly tell a mountain to jump and it would sail through air." Tio rode behind her in awe as he again wondered. Could she be the answer to his own prayers? Did he need to hold her at a distance now? His love for her grew, but he dared not risk losing her until he was sure.

Chapter 20

The ride back to Rustshade was far more enjoyable than the ride to meet the monks. On the way, Tiobald had seethed with anger, barked orders, and not spoken to her of what she did wrong. She wanted to please him, but he refused to tell her what he required.

Brother Joanis spoke amiably with her. "I have never seen anyone speak to Brother Sabistine as you did, sister." He chuckled softly. "We are not to revel in another's misfortune Scripture says." His laugh grew. "I will need to seek forgiveness before I lay my head down this night."

Esmeralda relaxed and smiled. "Some people can be utterly thick-headed. They get a notion lodged in their skull, and no amount of reason or proof to the contrary can dislodge it. However, you will find the men and women, though they be few, of Rustshade a most generous and hungry flock."

They neared the gate and Tiobald dashed ahead of them to enter first. "To God be the glory," he shouted.

A crowd quickly gathered. Dunlang spoke, his words breathless and eyes wide. "The monk agreed to bring blessings?"

Tiobald's voice boomed. "Lady Esmeralda has not only persuaded the good Brother Joanis to give blessing to our Wilm and Kel's babe, she has enticed him to live with us and instruct us."

The men gasped and muttered. In moments, chants of "Hazzah" and cheers of her name reverberated off the walls. Tiobald's chest couldn't be more swollen as he smiled at her.

Dunlang thrust out his hand to the monk, "Brother, you are the answer to scores of years of prayer. Come, I will show you our humble chapel and your home."

Newt took her horse when she dismounted as the men bowed and continued to cheer her. "Thank you, Lady Esmeralda."

"The Lord bless you, m'lady."

Tiobald stood and crossed his arms over his puffed chest with shoulders back. His face filled with a foolish grin. She steeled herself and inched toward him on halting steps as the crowd dispersed. Would he at last welcome her?

His gaze locked with hers and his smile remained.

She continued forward. A half dozen steps separated them.

"You are a wonder." His words were airy, breathless.

Four steps remained.

His smiled cracked. Fading with the setting sun.

Two steps.

His hands dropped to his sides and his brows pulled together.

She reached for him.

"Best see if the young monk requires any help. The chapel and the hermitage attached to it have not been used a great long time." He turned his back and strolled away.

Esmeralda swallowed her tears and followed.

Brother Joanis agreed with Esmeralda; the chapel would need to be cleaned before the blessing. Jeni and Heart arrived to help along with a smattering of men. While the women washed the surfaces, the men straightened the pews and made sure they were still sound. They repaired those that were in need. The baptismal font couldn't be located so the blacksmith went to work as the sun cast its last rays over the shire.

As the first stars blinked in the indigo sky, Esmeralda silently followed Tiobald to his home. His behavior didn't make it feel like she belonged within it. He held the door open for her. The crackling fire danced with vibrant yellows and oranges. He pulled a jug from the mantle and poured two drinks. He hadn't said a word and didn't now as he offered her a wooden cup.

She didn't take it. "What do you require of me?"

He stared at her, brows drawn together, the cup hanging between them. "'Tis a bit of libation after a long day."

"What do you expect of me here?"

He continued to stare.

"Am I supposed to cook your meals?"

Without spilling any liquid, he lowered the drink to his side. His words were heavy. "This is your home, Esmeralda. You are not a slave." He put both cups on the table and leaned back against it, arms and ankles crossed. "We will break the fast together. The men in Rustshade are well equipped to prepare a meal; it can be the task of whichever of us rises first. A group will set out on the morning's hunt. The majority of the remaining shire meets for the midday in the hall you were in for council. I have often dined with Dunlang for the evening meal." His head turned to look at her. "But now…"

Esmeralda nodded, but she still hadn't moved. "Understood. Morning and evening meals. Cleaning? Mending?"

"Esmeralda, what do *you* want from *me*? This is your home." He pointed to the table under the window. "I brought you all the information Rustshade has on herbs and healings."

She moved and brushed her fingers over the scrolls. "Healing. I will see to the healings of the shire. Mayhaps someone can read them to me. I never learned." She swallowed and whispered the next. "But you want nothing more?" She held her breath.

Tap, tap, tap. Tiobald reached for the latch without answering her.

"Blessings, m'lord, m'lady. I know you have worked hard with the monk you brought us," Jeni giggled. She held out a steaming pot. "I brought a stew to save you some time." Her cheeks pinked. "And I know you have other interests to see to this night." She giggled again. "Your first true night together."

Tiobald sat the pot on the larger table. "Thank you. You are ever thoughtful."

Esmeralda managed a thank you before he closed the door. He stood with his back to her leaning on the table both hands braced on either side of the pot. "Do you have other interests to see to, m'lord?" she whispered.

"Esmeralda, you have had a long day and longer night."

"Healing the town. I understand." Tears choked her words as she darted into the bedchamber.

Chapter 21

Tio begged her to eat something, but she cried inside the bedchamber for much of the night. He clenched and unclenched his fists until his arms ached. He desperately wanted to go to her, to hold and comfort her. But he knew what being that close to her, in the bedchamber, would do to him. He couldn't lose her. Not like he lost his mother and sister. Writhing in birth pains, screaming until they were hoarse. Then the silence. The heartbreaking silence.

He couldn't do that to Esmeralda. Not that beautiful creature who cut a living babe from his mother and helped them both to survive. Not the bold, confident, brilliant woman who talked a monk into coming and living amongst them. Not her. The entire shire needed her. He needed her. He would die before he ever let that kind of death come to her.

He stood at the cutboard slicing cheese when he heard her skirt swish. Today she wore purple. Her eyes were red and puffy. He set the trencher with the cheese and some bread on the table with Jeni's pot of stew he had warmed over the fire. He pulled out a chair and spoke softly. "Come, Esmeralda. Break the fast with me."

"I have no appetite." She reached for the latch.

He moved toward her. "When was the last time you ate?"

"At the celebration I assume was to commemorate my arrival."

"It was to laud our wedding."

"Wedding? We have no marriage." Her words were bitter and filled with pain.

"You are my wife, Esmeralda."

She turned. "Am I?" She took a step, her hand outstretched to brush his cheek.

He stepped back.

"You behave as if you never wanted to choose."

"I didn't."

Tio had hunted most of his life. He knew well the look of a mortally wounded animal pleading to be put out of its misery. Esmeralda bore that look. Her arm dropped to her side. The blacks of her eyes nearly disappeared in a sea of watery green.

She stared at him unblinking for another heartbeat, then turned and walked outside.

Tio crumbled into the chair, his head in his hands. As Rustshade's Second in command and the Administrator of Justice, he never lied. And he swore he would never lie to Esmeralda. But he'd been wrong. He had crushed her. Whatever there may have been between them, it would never be now. But he was Second, and Esmeralda was his wife. He loved her. He would always love her. Even when she hated him.

Esmeralda staggered from Tiobald's home. It was so much worse than she thought. He'd never wanted her. She looked to the gate. Should she leave? She couldn't find her way back to MeeMa on her own. Should she find another home within the walls? The hayloft of the stable? She'd slept in worse places.

"M'lady," Wilm bowed low and kissed her hand. Beside him, Kel carried their son. He pulled her close and kissed his wife's cheek. "Blessings on you, m'lady." He took his son from Kel and placed him in Esmeralda's arms.

"You wish me to…"

"There could be no other godmother for him."

"I'm honored."

"And we are doubly blessed." Wilm waved out an arm and they walked toward the chapel. They gathered at the steps outside.

Brother Joanis met them at the entrance. "I see we have his godmother and both parents. Are their others?"

Heart, Jeni and the men gathered around them. Two stepped forward and came beside her. A another man Esz didn't know and Tiobald. Had he just arrived or had he followed her?

"Is the child a boy or girl?"

"A boy," Esmeralda answered Joanis. As both midwife and godmother, it was her role.

"Has he been christened?"

"No, Brother Joanis."

"I bless you, son, in the name of the Father, and the Son, and the Holy Spirit." He dipped the little finger of his right hand in a brass bowl, then put his finger in the baby's mouth. Next, the monk waved them inside the chapel, and they walked to the front.

The room glistened. Brother Joanis must have stayed up all night to finish the work. A new wooden pedestal with a bronze basin on top sat filled with water.

She cradled the babe as he wiggled and yawned while the rest of Rustshade filled the pews. They creaked and groaned under the weight of so many.

"What name do you give the child?"

Esmeralda looked to Wilm. He smiled at her. "What was your father's name, m'lady?"

"Ido," she whispered.

Brother Joanis grinned. "A Hebrew name which means *to be mighty*. A fitting name for the first child to be born in Rustshade in many years. And what do you ask of the church?"

"The grace of Christ," Esmeralda said.

Brother Joanis looked to Wilm and Kel. "You have asked to have your child christened and blessed. In doing so, you are accepting the responsibility of training him in the practice of the faith. It will be your duty to bring him up to keep God's commandments, as Christ taught us, to love God and our neighbors. Do you clearly understand what you are undertaking?

Ido's parents spoke as one. "We do."

He now turned to Esmeralda and the two men who would also serve as godparents. "Are you ready to help Wilm and Kel, bearers of this child, in their duty as Christian parents?"

As they gave their pledge to help, she realized she could only fulfill the vow if she remained in Rustshade. Her choice had been made without really deciding.

Brother Joanis gathered the babe into his arms. "Ido, the Christian community welcomes you with great joy. In its name, I claim you for Christ our Savior by the sign of his cross." Joanis first poured a handful of water from the font over Ido's head, then he dipped his index finger in oil and traced a cross on the babe's forehead. "I further bless his parents." He marked each with an oily cross. "And his godparents." Esmeralda, Tiobald, and the other man were marked. "May God bless you and keep each of you in His holy care." He handed Ido back to Esmeralda.

Brother Joanis nodded to Esmeralda before he turned to the congregation. "I am most honored to have followed my Lord's example in blessing this child as well as his parents. Jesus admonished His disciples as to the importance of children in God's kingdom. 'And he took them up in his arms, put *his* hands upon them, and blessed them.' May this babe grow in the love and wisdom for the Lord and bless others as his very life has blessed Rustshade."

Brother Joanis fingered his beads as he looked out on his flock. "I was recently reminded of those words, and the importance of not just blessing new lives but all the faithful. I am honored to serve this community and bring God's Word and love more vividly before you."

He bowed his head but raised his hands to the heavens, "Let us pray. My dear brothers and sisters, let us ask our Lord Jesus Christ to look lovingly on this child who is christened Ido, on his parents, and godparents, and on all the faithful gathered here. Amen."

"Amen."

Esmeralda handed Ido back to his mother and the entire shire came forward to see him. The excitement in the room made it hum and vibrate against her skin. Tiobald stood beside her, his shoulders thrown back and chin high, and he gave her a nod and a smile.

How could he look so proud of her one moment, and yet so thoroughly reject her the next? The man made her head hurt.

Esmeralda noticed Kel's stance change. Her shoulders rounded, face reddened, breath more labored. She inched up behind Wilm and whispered in his ear. "Time to take them home, Wilm. Don't overtax them on their first day out."

He took his son and wrapped a steadying, strong, and protective arm around his wife. Esmeralda's heart ached. A longing sprang up in her when Kel laid her head on Wilm's shoulder as they walked home. Why was that simple jester too much to ask of her own husband?

Chapter 22

Esmeralda followed Wilm's family home and checked on Kel's sutures. A few spots concerned her. She snatched up a pitcher and headed for the gate.

"Esmeralda." Tiobald stepped in her path. "Where are you going?"

"To the stream."

"We have collected plenty of water."

"Yes, but I need leeches."

His nose wrinkled and he stepped back. "By the sword, what for?"

"Why does it matter? You have assigned me the task of healer. I need them to fulfill my duty to the shire."

She tried to side-step him.

He blocked her. "You are my wife, and I will see to your care." He snatched the pitcher from her hand. "Newt." He handed the young man the container. "Esmeralda needs leeches."

"M'lady?"

She sighed, her empty fist on her hip. "Kel's wound has spots that are not mending well. The leeches will bring fresh blood back to the site, speed healing, and prevent disease from setting in."

With wide-eyes, Newt nodded.

"If you would please collect three for me. No." She chewed on her lower lip. If she collected them, she would choose them according to her particular needs. It would be impossible to explain to Newt, who obviously didn't want the job in the first place. "Collect a dozen."

"You want a dozen leeches. Aye, m'lady."

He turned toward the gate looking a little unsteady.

"Thank you," she called after him.

"Now, let us go to midday, Esmeralda." Without touching her, Tiobald escorted her to the same room where she had testified before the council. Now tables filled the open place where she'd stood and a third chair waited at the high table.

Esmeralda turned to join Heart and Jeni as they served.

"No, Esmeralda. Come."

"I can help."

"As wife of the Second, you'll join us as your station dictates."

My station? She bit down on her tongue and climbed the three steps ahead of her dictator of a husband—who refused to be a husband. "Good day to you, Lord Dunlang," she said in the sweet tone she used to get her way with MeeMa.

"Good day, m'lady."

"I was just telling Tiobald, how I wished to lend a hand with Jeni and Heart. With two women indisposed, it has left them shorthanded."

"A great idea, m'lady. You are ever helpful."

She shot Tiobald a smug smirk and hurried toward the women snatching up trays and delivering them to the long boards.

When everyone was served, she trudged up the steps again and took her place at the end of the table with the two men. Tiobald handed her a tray with venison and boar, she took a couple thin slices adding some of Jeni's vegetables and a slice of dark bread. She nibbled slowly. She knew she needed sustenance, and it was pleasing enough to the tongue, but she had no appetite. Who could eat next to a man who refused to really talk to her, didn't want her as his wife, and only wished to parade her around and glory in her successes? Why? What did he gain by playing the dutiful husband, marrying her in the sight of God and before his friends, but never fulfilling his husbandly duties? Was there something wrong with him? A deformity. An inability?

"Esmeralda?"

She blinked, trying to bring Tiobald's beard-covered face into focus.

"Dunlang asked you a question."

She looked past Tiobald to the older man. "Sorry, m'lord. I lost myself in thought. What did you say?"

"Are you not enjoying your meal?"

She glanced at her trencher. She'd moved the food around but not eaten much. "Yes, m'lord, it is good. I—"

"I imagine 'tis quite a change to come to a new home and be married so suddenly. Your arrival has been more eventful than most." Dunlang chuckled and raised his tankard to her in salute. "We have been more than blessed, but you haven't had a quiet moment. Things should settle now. Kel and Ido are doing well, and Olva's babe is not expected until winter. Thankfully, we men rarely need a healer's touch." He hoisted the tankard again.

"Thank you, m'lord, I'm sure I will find my equilibrium soon." She offered him a quick smile and tried to concentrate on her food. She managed a few more bites before scooping up her own trencher, along with others from the high table, as she helped clean.

"Are you hale, Esmeralda?" Tiobald came to her elbow, scrunched brows forming a furrow. She continued to help clear the tables.

"As well as a woman in my particular situation can expect to be, m'lord." She offered him a quick curtsy and returned to her work.

Jeni met her in the narrow kitchen that sat alongside the common chamber. "You look tired, my friend." She took the stack of trenchers from Esmeralda and carried them to the large basin filled with water.

Esmeralda leaned a hip against the long cutboard on one side of the room and smiled.

"What are you grinning at?" Jeni giggled. "You look like a cat who has eaten a favorite pet. Did your husband keep you up all night?"

"It has been long since anyone called me a friend. Thank you."

"You are the best thing to come to this little shire in all the time I have been here. Kel…" She glanced around and whispered. "… and Heart are nice enough. But they are not like you. You…" She stopped and stared off at nothing. "You are…" She shrugged and giggled as she glanced back. "… perfectly you."

"I noticed you didn't mention Olva."

"Augh, *that* woman!" She stuck her tongue out. "Clearly you know her and that she is never kind."

"Where is she? She isn't still confined to her home?"

"Nay." She covered her giggle with a wet hand. "After her outburst with you, Lord Tio forbid her to return to the common meal until she could hold her tongue. Apparently, she has not yet found her self-restraint. Not that she has ever had any. Oooh, she is a nit!"

Esmeralda caught Jeni in a one-armed hug. "Thank you, my friend. Let's finish these dishes and visit your garden."

"Will we be having company?" Jeni tipped her chin toward Tiobald who sat in the other room talking with the last few stragglers. His gaze landed on her from time to time.

"He doesn't seem to like me out of his sight."

Jeni elbowed her with a giggle, her cheeks pinked. "Love. I've never seen Lord Tio so out of sorts. You've had a powerful effect on him."

Esmeralda stared back at him. She definitely had an effect on the man. But it most assuredly was not love. The little bit of food in her belly soured and burned the back of her throat. It was long past time that she locked away the hope that had sprang up in her four days ago when she hadn't been sacrificed but married to the most gorgeous man she'd ever seen. Whatever end was to come for her, it would be alone—as she had known from the day her father died.

She swiped at the last tear she would cry over the man who did not love her and turned to the task of cleaning beside her chatty, kind *friend.*

Chapter 23

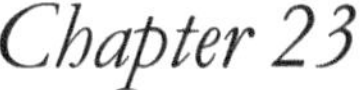

Tio didn't like the way Esmeralda got along with Jeni. Well, that wasn't entirely true. He clenched and unclenched his fists and rolled his shoulders. Jeni was a fine woman. Zeke had chosen well. Esmeralda needed other women around her, especially with how things were between them. But she smiled and even laughed as they talked on the way to the garden. Esmeralda was different with him. He had no one to blame but himself.

Tio kept his distance as they talked and giggled. His chest tightened until he was sure he'd never draw another breath. After a time, they strolled back toward the square and Jeni led her to the tanner's before turning toward home. He stormed in after Esmeralda when she boldly walked into the shop alone. She was a brazen thing. No concept that she belonged to him.

Her beautiful face scrunched in confusion. "M'lord?"

He hated that she called him by his title and not his name. She, above all, should… a moment of clarity struck him, and he remembered she'd wanted an apron to protect her gowns. He forced his fists to unclench and drew air into his constricted chest. "Forgive my delay, Lew. Esmeralda had an item she wished to request of you."

After a quick glance between the couple, Lew bowed. "It would be my honor, m'lady. Might I make you some boots or slippers?"

"That is kind of you, Lew, but what I really need is an apron." Lew stared for a moment while she described the specifics of the piece she needed.

Lew nodded and handed Tio a strip of leather with markings at regular intervals. "If you would measure your lady wife in these areas." Lew picked up a bit of coal and piece of parchment.

Tio stood unable to move, and Esmeralda snatched the measuring strip from him, "The heavens forbid you should be forced to touch me," she muttered so quietly Tio barely heard her. She reported the figures of the length she wanted, the dimension around her hips and bosom, and the width of the skirt portion.

"Very well, a couple of days and I should have the newest hide ready to fashion into what you desire."

"Thank you, Lew," she said.

Tio followed Esmeralda outside. "I agreed to meet Jeni in her home, if I am allowed to go." Her words were soft and tentative.

"I have not forbidden you anything."

She pulled up short and stared at him. After a moment, she shook her head and turned toward her friend's house. "I'll be at your house before evening meal."

Tio stood watching the pleasing swing of her slender hips. His heart ached though, for she didn't view where she lived as her home. In truth, he knew he had done nothing to make her welcome. His fists clenched and unclenched repeatedly. How could he make her believe she was wanted when he was terrified his love would kill her?

"M'lord?"

Tio turned to Newt. "Aye."

"'Tis time for the judgments you scheduled prior to going on the Blessed Choosing."

The petty squabbles of men with no women to temper them. But what of Esmeralda? He needed to watch over her. She didn't know the proper way to comport herself around men. Fist clenching, he closed his eyes for a moment. "Newt, I need you to watch over Esmeralda. She is… unaccustomed to our ways, and I don't wish anyone to think less of her by her innocent actions."

"Of course, m'lord."

"She's at Jeni's home. Zeke should still be out on the hunt."

Newt inclined his head and strolled off. Tio had sent him. He had no reason to resent Newt. But he did. He hated the thought of any other man near her.

Tio entered his home to find it filled with an odd aroma. Not unpleasant, but not completely appetizing either. A pot hung over the flames of a well-built fire. Esmeralda sat stitching a length of heavy cloth. He didn't know what to say to her, so he walked to the pot. It looked better than it smelled.

"You will have to be patient with me, m'lord."

Even in his own home she refused to call him by his Christian name. His fist clenched again.

"Always, Esmeralda. I am not overly hungry at the moment."

"Well, you may be less so when you try to eat my cooking."

It was a simple, calm statement that caused him to turn and look at her.

She didn't glanced up. "I never learned to cook—food. Ointment, elixirs, teas, tinctures, I can near do in my sleep. But MeeMa saw that I ate one meal a day."

Only one meal? Well, that explained a few things.

"Her fare was always simple—nothing like you are used to here. Jeni has agreed to instruct me. And Lord willing, I won't poison either of us before I acquire a knack for it."

"Lord willing," he actually chuckled. The woman was honest to a fault. It made him love her all the more.

Her nose crinkled and she jumped up. "Does it smell burnt?"

"Mayhaps a little."

"Oh, goose feathers to the highest heavens." She reached for the pot. Tio snatched back her hand. She stared where his hand encircled her wrist, but she didn't pull away.

He released her. "Careful, or you'll be burned as well." He took a thick bit of cloth from the mantle, removed the pot. and placed it on the cutboard.

She scooped some into two bowls and set them on the table. His was nearly full. Hers had barely three spoons full.

"You don't eat enough, Esmeralda."

"With my cooking, you may not either."

He smiled as they sat in silence. She continued to sew whatever she was working on, and they let the steaming brew cool.

It was far from the best meal he had ever eaten, but it was also nowhere near the worst. He told her as much.

She just shrugged. "It should get better." She rinsed their dishes and looked to the pot. "Should I throw out the rest?"

"It was not that bad."

Again, she shrugged. At the doorway to the bedchamber she stopped. Holding to the doorframe she took a deep breath and slowly stepped inside. "Rest you well, m'lord."

"Rest you well, Esmeralda." She clearly didn't want to retire, but she didn't want to stay talking with him either. He leaned his forearms on his thighs, fists clenching until his arms and shoulders ached. He had made a right awful mess of things. And he had utterly no idea how to fix them without risking her life and his heart.

Chapter 24

Esmeralda rose from the place that tore her heart from her chest. A marriage bed was meant to be shared. Another gown lay draped over the bench at the foot of the oversized furniture. Bright yellow with red trim. She slipped it over her head and secured her belt. It took a while to unbraid her hair, brush it and re-plait it before winding it at the base of her skull. It was the proper way for a married woman to wear their locks. But she resented doing it.

Tiobald entered the common living area with an armful of wood at the same moment she emerged from the hated bedchamber. They inclined their heads toward one another.

"Do you want me to heat some of last eve's slop or would you prefer cheese and bread?" She cut off his response as she continued. "Jeni has promised to teach me to make porridge but I need to know if you prefer it sweet or savory?" She hadn't realized there was more than one way to make a morning gruel.

He smiled, "I will gladly eat it anyway you prefer, if you will join me in breaking the fast each morn."

"I'll get Jeni's advice. But for this day?"

"Cheese is fine."

She unwrapped the block and cut them several slices. She gave most of it to him. Food still was not setting well in her anxious belly, and last night's disaster had done nothing to improve the situation.

"I do not require a new gown every day."

"You are of the household of the Second. Your station—"

"Seems to be indulgent and wasteful. *I* don't require a new one regardless of the station's requirements."

Tiobald considered her. "As you wish."

"Might I be allowed to hang a few rods for drying of herbs?" She pointed to the open space to the left of the bedchamber.

"This is your home, Esmeralda. Do as you see fit." He offered her another tentative smile. "I'm part of the hunt today. If all goes well, I should be back for midday."

She nodded her understanding.

"Newt will be near if you need anything."

The watchdog left a guard to control her? He was a possessive man for someone who wanted nothing to do with her. "As you wish," she repeated his words.

They left the house in separate directions, without farewells or blessings.

Esmeralda went to the chapel first. She needed some instruction at the early gathering Brother Joanis offered to any who wished to learn. Mayhaps it would give her a softening of her rapidly hardening heart. There could be no better place than God's house.

Calmer for her time in the holy place, she checked on Kel. The leeches had done their work. The new mother wouldn't need much more of her assistance. She needed to find something to fill her days—and quickly.

With Newt's help she gathered some relatively straight, long branches, a ball of twine, a handful of nails, and a hammer. He carried them back to her door but wouldn't enter. She took them and dropped them on the little table with the parchments. Newt adamantly refused to come inside and assist her.

"It is wholly improper for me, a single man, to be in a married man's home alone with his wife.

Esmeralda sighed and pulled over the sturdiest of Tiobald's chairs. She took the two cuffs she had finally finished sewing last eve and slid them over her arms. They were already tied at her wrist, and with the long dangling sleeves of her gown contained inside, she only required someone to tie them just below her elbows.

She stepped outside. "Newt, are you allowed to assist me with this?" Esmeralda showed him what she needed. He turned three shades of red but secured the top of the forearm guards.

With hammer in hand, she pounded four nails into the ceiling beams, and tied two lengths of twine to both. One long and one short so more herbs could hang in the confined space. They would have to duck under the lower ones but hopefully, Tiobald wouldn't mind.

Esz moved to strike another pair of nails into the ceiling placing one foot on the strong edge of the chair and the other on the top slat in the back for added reach. She balanced precariously. Holding one nail between her lips she pinched the other between her finger and thumb and swung the hammer.

"Esmeralda!"

She startled at the shout from behind her. The hammer fell grazing her forehead. Nails clinked on the floor. Her arms extended to regain her balance. She yelped and fell backwards, landing safely in Tiobald's arms.

"By the sword woman, what are you doing?"

She leapt from his grasp, brushed her forehead checking for blood. Only a couple drop of red showed on her fingers. She stared at him one fist perched on a hip, "You said this very morn, I could string drying racks for my herbs."

His scowl was deep, and his fists clenched and unclenched in a wild rhythm. "You should not be doing it alone."

"You didn't offer to do it. And Newt refused to be in the room with me."

"It is not proper—"

She stomped up to him. "Then there is something you need to be aware of. I have treated many patients. Women, children, boys and *men*. Alone. In their homes. I frequented the tavern and spoke to the merchants who gathered there."

His eyes grew wide, his mouth agape.

"Yet, I came to you a maiden. Not that it matters to you." She brushed off her hands and eased back into her slippers. Her head shot up. "Wait… you're back. What time is it?"

"The midday is about to begin."

"Goose feathers to the highest heaven." She flew out the door. "I promised Jeni I would arrive early to help prepare."

She barely heard him call her name as she pulled her hem up high and ran for the common building.

Chapter 25

Tio reeled in Esmeralda's wake. He'd done everything to protect her, and it had only left her to struggle alone. Had he not caught her, she would have smacked her head against the table before landing on the hard worn floorboards. Seeing her teeter awkwardly on the chair made his blood turn to ice.

Then she burst from his arms rather than lingering in his comfort. He'd pushed her so far away that she now didn't want his touch. He dropped into the chair she'd toppled from and held his head.

Esmeralda told him boldly of the men she'd attended without proper escort. She wasn't from his world. Abandoned to her own devices meant frequenting a tavern if need be. No honor was afforded her so she never feared ruining her reputation. But Rustshade was different. With so few women, there were things that just weren't done.

But how did he rein in her free spirit without crushing it? How did he go about explaining to the men he would one day rule, that his wife would not behave as their wives were expected?

The throb in his head rattled his entire body.

He'd been late to the meal, and Esmeralda already sat picking at her meager portion. She really needed to eat more. Before everyone had finished, she again joined the women in the kitchen area. He could hear her laughing from where he sat.

"Things do not look to be going well between you." Dunlang leaned back in his chair and enjoyed his ale. "I know you fought long and hard not to participate in the choosing."

"We have been cruel and near evil to bring women here knowing they would die from our love."

"But she is different." Dunlang raised his tankard in Esmeralda's direction as she swept through the room clearing tables. "You have received an amazing blessing, Tio."

"You think I don't see that?"

"I don't know what to think. You show the woman no affection. And I am concerned about her. I can't prove it, and I don't want to know, but I do not believe you have enjoyed union with that wonderful woman. Women are not like us, Tio. They require a bond—a connection with other people. The strongest of those ties is with a husband. Deny her that, under some misguided sense of protecting her, and you'll destroy her as surely as if she'd died in childbirth."

"Dunlang, I…"

The older man stood and thumped Tio on the shoulder as he passed. "The blight that took our women has been lifted. The well destroyed. Our new beginning is taking shape. Even Kel dined with us this day—babe in her arm. Love her, Tio. The future is bright."

Dunlang bowed to Esmeralda before handing her his tankard. They spoke for a moment and she smiled at him. Her gaze lighted on Tio for just a moment as she returned to her self-assigned task. A hollow sadness met his smile. Their chance might already have passed.

Tio's duties and the dressing of the game they brought back kept him occupied for the remainder of the day. Newt leaned against Tio and Esmeralda's home when he returned.

The young man nodded and pushed off the wall. "Rest you well, m'lord."

He disappeared before Tio could reply. He waited outside, his heart pounding. *Lord, help me make things right with her.* Opening the door, an aroma, more pleasant than last night, overwhelmed him. Esmeralda stirred the pot over a much smaller flame.

"Fare thee well, Esmeralda."

His odd cheerful greeting made her turn and stare at him. Her narrow brows pinched together. "Are you hale?"

Not the response he'd hoped for. "Aye. Whatever you are making smells good."

She turned back to the pot and stirred. "As I said, couldn't get much worse than last night. Jeni tried to point out where I'd faltered. I try not to make the same mistake more than once."

"Always a good goal." She only nodded. Tio didn't know how to keep their stilted conversation going. He noted that three rows of nails now adorned his ceiling. Each held two branches; one came to just above her head, and the other lower, almost at the height of her waist. Tucked so far to one end of the room, it was an efficient system that maximized the vertical area without encroaching on the living space.

"Is there a problem?" She followed his gaze. "I can remove them—"

"'Tis more than fine. Did you finish it alone?"

"I have done things alone most of my life. 'Tis often the easiest and fastest way to get a matter completed." She snatched up a bowl and ladled it full of the stew. "Well, I think 'tis ready. Though with my cooking skills, that may not be a good thing."

She prepared a small portion for herself and sat across from him, lifting a spoon tentatively.

"Thank you, Esmeralda."

The spoon hung in midair. "Whatever for?"

He pushed a smile to his lips. "For all that you do. For trying when things don't come easy. For not running screaming from me when I chose you. For being kind in the face of adversity. I regret that I have made things difficult for you."

She shrugged. "My life before coming here was full of *adversity*, as you say. I have been well trained to keep my head up." She ate her paltry portion, and rose to rinse her bowl. "Sleep you well, m'lord."

She turned and opened the door to the central unused bedchamber. He glanced around her. Many things he no longer used, and had tossed aside, were now neatly stacked. A bedroll lay in the empty space on the floor.

He jumped from his chair toppling it with a bang. "What are you doing?" He voice was far harsher than he'd intended.

She cringed. "It hurts to sleep in the other chamber."

"If the mattress is uncomfortable, I can—"

"The bed is the most luxurious I have ever experienced. But it is a marriage bed. A place not meant to be enjoyed alone. It tears at my heart to be reminded every night that I am not wanted here."

"Esmeralda." He moved toward her, but she shrank from him.

"I have slept in drafty haylofts and out of doors in the rain. This is warm and dry. The bedroll was comfortable on the journey here. It will serve me well."

He reached for her hand. Their fingers brushed but she wouldn't let him hold on to her. "You are wanted, Esmeralda."

Her eyes swam in tears. "Your words this night have been sweet, but your actions have made matters more than clear. I know what is expected of me and what is not." She turned, took a step inside the room, and paused. "If you should ever change your mind…" She looked at him. A brow arched. Uncomfortable silence hung between them. The door closed.

He'd failed again. He could have taken her into his arms. But fear rooted him to the floor. He picked put his cup and raised it above his head. To hurl it against the wall would only upset her more. He slammed it down on table with a *thunk* and drew in a deep breath.

Chapter 26

Tio stirred from his place before the hearth as Esmeralda emerged from her new bedchamber, again dressed in the purple gown. She considered him for a moment as he stretched and worked the stiffness from his muscles.

"You do not favor sleeping alone in a marriage bed either." She turned to the cutboard. "There is always the other chamber, but I couldn't get the door open."

"No one goes in there." His barked caused her to jump. His fists clenched as he fought to rein in his outbursts. "I'll be fine. If you sleep on the floor, then so shall I."

Her next words were muttered and most likely not intended for him to hear. "No point in both of us being miserable." She sighed. "If you wish porridge, I'll need to stoke the fire."

"I'll do it." He stomped out to collect wood. When the flames came to life, she hung the smallest of his pots over them. He tried to reach for her hand but she turned away without noticing.

"I'm going to the chapel."

"What of your meal?"

Her nose crinkled. "I've never liked the mush. Mother told MeeMa even as a child I'd spit it out before she could get it fully in my mouth."

"There is cheese and bread, as always."

"You're running low on both. You enjoy them. Bread is the next thing Jeni will attempt to teach me."

"I'll get some cheese from Yip. He keeps the shire well supplied."

She nodded and slipped out the door.

Tio glanced around his home as he plopped into a chair. With the exception of the drying racks hanging empty and the organized center bedchamber, his house hadn't changed with Esmeralda's arrival. She still didn't view it as her home. She'd again voiced her belief that she was unwanted. And, as in the past score of years, he ate alone.

Esmeralda strolled toward the gate with a basket over her arm. Tio came beside her. "Where are you going?"

"To gather herbs."

Tio stepped in front of her, pulled her up short, and shook his head.

"This is my job. A healer needs herbs."

"You are my wife—"

She stepped in close, her voice a harsh whisper. "No, I am NOT. You have allowed me to be the town's healer, and I must have herbs to do it. Without this single task, I will waste away without a purpose."

Tio started to wave at Newt, but she smacked at his hand.

"Newt can't do this. I must know what grows here about. What will I find in abundance, and what will I have to acquire through trade or purchase? From some plants I collect the leaves, others the stems, and others the roots. Gathering the wrong portion can be deadly. No one can do this but me." She leaned back with her arms crossed to lock the basket out of his reach. "Do enemy soldiers roam the woods?"

"Nay."

"Wild beasts pose a danger?"

"Boars."

"I know how to deal with boar. If there is nothing else, you are left with these options, m'lord. Allow me to do my assigned job alone as I always have, send Newt as my *nursemaid*, or accompany me yourself. But I tell you true. I *will* be collecting herbs today."

Others started to stare. Tio waved allowing her to proceed. "Let us go."

A curt nod came before her stomped steps.

"M'lady! Lady Esmeralda!" They turned at Jeni's shouts. She seized Esmeralda's forearms. "Esz, 'tis Olva. The birth pains have begun."

Esmeralda's shoulders sagged. "She will not allow me to aid her." Her words were quiet, etched with pain.

"But the babe."

She sighed and thrust the basket at Jeni. "Hold this and do *not* give it to *him*." Her finger wagged in his direction. She didn't leave until Jeni nodded. "I'll be back in a moment."

Jeni's weight shifted several times; she didn't dare look at him. If he asked, he had no doubt she would relinquish the item.

Esmeralda returned shortly with an earthenware jug hooked on her finger. "Give this to her husband. She is to drink all of it, but he is never to tell her where it came from."

"You aren't coming?"

"I could do no more even if Olva allowed my presence. 'Tis far too soon for the babe to survive should it persist in coming. I'll return in a few hours. We'll know one way or the other the child's fate by then."

Jeni squeezed her hand. "Are you hale, Esz?"

She gave a slim nod. "Take that to Olva. I'll be praying."

Esmeralda's steps were slow—heavy. Once outside the gate, Esmeralda walked to a clearing and faced the sun. She raised her head to the heavens, and closed her eyes. She remained still for some time. Her shoulders slipped from their high perch near her ears, hands relaxed at her side, breaths slow and deep. When she began moving again, her head was down likely searching the ground for anything she might use.

Tio followed at a close distance. He wanted her to remain at ease, and his presence did not avail her of such.

In the meadow south of the gate, she removed her slippers and knotted her hem in a few places raising it to above her ankles. Not appropriate, but no one was here to judge—except him. She skipped and twirled. She even hummed as her basket filled.

As the midday passed his stomach growled, while she continued as if hunger never touched her. She ducked and picked a mushroom. Her hair snarled on a low-slung branch when she rose. She pulled it free, sat down her herbs, and undid her braid. Her hair fell in rich red waves almost to her knees. His hands ached from wanting to be buried within what looked like velvet. Wisps, like dancing flames, fluttered about her face.

Having almost circled the shire, she set down the burgeoning basket and turned to the heavens once more. After several minutes she sighed and began to re-braid her hair.

"I like it down." Tio said from where he stood several steps away.

"Is not *proper* for a married woman." She threw his word back.

"As you continue to remind me, you do not believe we are married."

"I hardly want the entire shire to bear witness to my shame."

As he stepped closer, she finished winding the plait at the base of her head and secured it with two smooth polished sticks. "There is no shame for you, Esmeralda." He wished he could call her Esz too, but feared it was a name reserved for friends. And he was not amongst their number. "If anyone has cause for guilt, 'tis me."

She stilled, her gaze searching his face.

"I have not behaved as a husband should. I have made you feel poorly when I wanted only to honor and care for you."

She retrieved her basket and moved toward the gate. "But not to love."

Tio groaned. Nothing he did was right. He loved her so much it made him a complete fool.

Chapter 27

"Esz. M'lady." Jeni quickly corrected before Esmeralda and Tio had fully cleared the gate. "Olva is demanding to see you. She has been screeching your name for the last hour."

Tio worried Esmeralda would collapse, she sagged so. But she passed her basket to Newt. "Would you deliver this to Tiobald's home, please?"

"Of course, m'lady."

They followed Jeni without a word. As they came to Dan and Olva's door "ES-MER-AL-DA!" rang through the air.

Esmeralda trembled and gripped the doorframe to steady herself. She took a deep breath before entering and crossing to the bedchamber. She stood in the doorway waiting. Her words were soft, and quaking. "I am here, Olva. There is no reason to scream like a banshee."

Dan paced around the living chamber while Tio stayed close to his wife, though he didn't enter the inner chamber.

"You! You horrid, ve-geful …" She knew better than defy Tio's order and call his wife a witch again. "I told you never to give me your poissson."

Esmeralda stood stiff, hands clasped before her, shoulders scrunched tight. Tio wasn't sure she breathed—her frame was so tight. "Was not poison, or you'd be dead. Clearly you are alive and well."

"I'm drunk!"

"Yes."

"You want me to be a blundering fool? Bring the sssame ssshame to my name as you have assuredly taken pride in all your life? Otherwissse, you would have ssstopped consssorting with that witch and behaved as any reasssonable person would. Well, will not work. I'm loved here."

Esmeralda only nodded.

"I warned you after you killed my dear mother, never would I take anything from you. And you sssneak it to my husssband like the sssnake you are."

Esmeralda placed her hand on Tio's chest preventing him from storming into the bedchamber and choking the life from Olva. His fists clenched and unclenched, and he moved away from the chamber door to pace with Dan. "I have not treated you, Olva. I aided your unborn babe. I would never allow your innocent child to suffer because of the hatred you bear against me."

"You wanted my baby drunk? How wicked can you be?"

"It was to stop the labor pains." Esmeralda's head rose slightly. "Have they ceased?"

"Aye." The word was offered begrudgingly. "Am I to ssstay drunk for the next three monthsss?" Olva's tone made Eseralda sigh.

"No, that would be even more harmful."

"Well, doesssn't matter. I'll not allow the woman who killed my mother to tend me and my babe."

"She refused to allow MeeMa or I to aid her. She could have been saved had you called us sooner. Don't make her mistake. There will come a point when nothing I do will help."

"She will not be making such foolish decisions." Dan stormed around Esmeralda and into the room. Tio came forward resting a hand on the small of Esmeralda's back. Dan looked at his wife. "I am your husband, woman. And the babe you carry is my blood. I'll not have you put my beloved offspring in jeopardy for some petty squabble you have with this fine woman."

"Fine woman! You don't know—"

"I know my Second has chosen her. I know Kel and Ido are more than hale. I watch m'lady joyfully serve at midday without the complaining or grumbling that accompanies any task you are asked to do. And, as wife of the Second, m'lady is not supposed to lower herself to such menial tasks. She does it out of the goodness of her heart. It was out of that same goodness she worked to save our babe. And, Wife, she will continue to do so until *I* say otherwise. You fight me on this, and I will strap you to that bed until m'lady brings the child forth hale. Then I will send you away never to hold him or see either of us again."

Esmeralda quaked against Tio's hand. "Surely, Olva is as eager to bear a healthy babe as you, sir. There should be no need to treat her so harshly."

Dan looked at Esmeralda with wide eyes. "There must be a little of the saint in you, m'lady, for you to seek to protect a woman who has treated you so horridly."

She shook her head. "Olva loved her mum dearly. I cannot fault her the pain she has suffered."

"But you lost both mother *and* your father," Tio said. "And yet you have a kind and tender heart."

Olva's sniffles filled the room. "You don't know what sh-sh-she's done. The manner of woman sh-sh-she is."

"I say she is far better than you!" Dan said causing his wife's tears to intensify.

"Please, do not continue to upset her. The pains may return."

"*We* will do whatever you require. Is that not true, Wife?"

Olva nodded weakly.

"If you gentleman would give us a moment, and Olva will allow it, I'd like to check the babe."

"She *will* allow it." Dan clomped into the living chamber following Tio.

Esmeralda closed the door only to emerge a few minutes later.

"What is required?" Dan stood in a wide stance with his arms crossed.

"The libation has done its work to calm the pains. She should stay abed for this night, and participate in only minimal activity until we are sure they will not return. Should they return, she may be required to stay abed for the remainder. It would not be best for Olva, but may be the only thing to save the babe."

"I will see everything is done as you instruct. And I'll inform Heart to come stay with her when I am not here." He stepped forward and took a knee. "I humbly beg your forgiveness for my wife's inexcusable behavior. I swear it is no reflection on your outstanding character. And I vow it will never happen again."

"I do not blame you, sir. The wounds between us are old, and the scars—ill healed." She turned and stepped outside. Her arms hugged tight about her.

Tio opened his arms. She didn't step into his embrace but, still rubbing her arms, she leaned forward and rested her forehead against his chest. He caressed her back in gentle strokes. "You are a kind woman, Esmeralda. You wished nothing but her best as she spit in your face. Not many could have been so compassionate in the face of such hatred. I certainly couldn't."

"Esz, m'lady. Oh, no." Jeni bit on her knuckles. "Tell me, they still live—well, the babe at least," she whispered.

Esmeralda straightened; her arms still tight about her. "Everyone lives."

"Oh, praise the Lord's mighty name."

"I was just going to take Esmeralda home. She hasn't eaten all day."

Jeni threw her arm around Esmeralda. "By the saints, you poor thing. You are coming to our home for the evening meal." She looked over her shoulder. "The both of you. Can't expect you to make a meal when you're all but shattered."

"I'm not really hungry."

"Don't want to hear another word. We have to get some food in you." Jeni all but dragged her home. "Zeke, grab the extra chairs. Lord Tio and Lady Esz dine with us tonight."

Zeke's head shot up, but after a moment he smiled. "Then our meal will be doubly blessed. Come friends, you are welcome here."

Tio chastised himself. Why could he not have managed to give her such warm or hospitable greeting to her own home? He needed to do something—anything to make her feel she belonged here, with him.

Chapter 28

Esmeralda didn't want to eat, and she certainly didn't want to socialize. Weary to the bone, she was sure she'd spent an entire week trying to escape a crazed bear.

But something had changed, this evening Tio had been sweet. The charge to defend her against Olva's attack. The steadying hand on her back. The tender embrace. The kind words. The man acted as though he wanted and cared about her in one moment and quite the contrary in the next. Thinking of him added to the ache in her head.

Jeni did most of the talking, and before the meal concluded, the weight of her time with Olva lifted. She laughed for a time sitting in Zeke and Jeni's warm home. Though structurally like Olva's or even Tio's, Jeni's house drew Esz in. Whether it was the flowers she'd dried and pressed before arranging them artfully on the wall, or the curtains of bright fabric to cover the windows, joy could be found in every corner. She was sad to leave, and return to Tio's stark house. More a monastery cell than a home. What she could do to make it feel more welcoming?

As they slipped out into the chill evening, she again hugged her arms.

Tio brushed against her. "I'll get you a cloak before the winter sets in." He stopped to grab wood as she went inside.

She passed through to her bedchamber, opened the door, and pulled up short. A narrow, raised bed with a billowing mattress and layers of blankets sat where the bedroll had been. She looked at him as he tended the fire.

"I couldn't bear the thought of you lying on the floor."

"Thank you. It is most kind." She stood still for a moment. "Rest you well—Tio."

He smiled wide and cheerful. "Rest you well, Esz."

She returned his smile "How do I go about acquiring a bath?"

"There is a communal bathing hall for our women. Jeni can show it to you."

"Lew should be finished with my apron."

"I'll collect it before I leave."

He did not say where he went, and Esmeralda did not ask as she slipped into her bed. Did he want to provide this for her out of kindness? Mayhaps things were not as they appeared with Tio, Second and sheriff of Rustshade. *Lord, please let it be so.*

All of Esmeralda's hopes for something more than mere peace between them were short lived. "Good morn, Esz."

"Good morn, Tio. Porridge?"

"Nay."

"Was it not to your liking?" Could she do nothing right for the man?

He laughed softly. "In truth, I have never favored the gruel much myself either. Cheese and bread will serve fine."

"With the herb collection and Olva," a shudder washed over her again. "I have yet to acquire the bread making skills. Mayhaps eggs?"

He stood and walked slowly toward her. "I do not believe you harmed Olva's mother. You do not need to fear her."

She turned away to hide her shame. "I do not fear her. She can make my standing with you no worse."

Tio sighed strong enough for his breath to warm her neck. His footfalls moved away. "I have some tasks to attend outside the shire.

Newt is here should you have need. A pleasant day to you, Esz." The door latched behind him before she could respond.

The weight of her loneliness almost drove Esmeralda to her knees. Tears no longer came. She straightened and turned to her herbs. Arranging them to dry would occupy the time until she was required to visit Olva again. Such a visit would stir her guilt until it became too much to bear. And today, no one would be there to lend his strength.

Chapter 29

The entire shire was quiet when she slipped from Tio's home, but Newt fell into step behind her. She walked in silence to Olva's. Dan stepped outside with Newt when she entered.

"Come to torture me again?"

"Have the pains returned?" Esmeralda asked without coming near her bed.

"No."

Esmeralda drew in a deep breath, releasing it slowly. "May I—"

"You know good and well I don't want anything from you and I don't want to ever look on your wicked face. As well as you know I can say nothing against you. How is it you have captured the sway of the Second and my own husband?"

Esmeralda opened her mouth.

Olva threw up her hand and turned away. "I don't want to know what horrid spell you have cast upon these fine men. Just be gone and tell my husband you don't need to return."

"But the babe …"

"He is doing fine as am I."

Esmeralda turned. Outside Dan held her gaze. "Is all well?"

"As far as I can determine."

"She refused you again." Dan's features hardened and his limbs went rigid. "Please come with me, m'lady." She followed him back inside the house and Newt trailed them.

"Olva!"

She trembled looking up at him from the flat of her back. A glare darted toward Esmeralda. "You hateful cur."

Dan drew back to slap her, but Esmeralda stayed his hand. "Peace, sir. Do not harm her."

"Do you see this woman? She will not speak against you, and now she saves you from the punishment you have rightly earned. When Lord Tiobald learns that you have again slandered his wife, what do you think with happen to you?"

Olva's gaze narrowed on Esmeralda, challenging her. "She wouldn't dare say a word against me after all she has done to me."

Dan gripped his wife by her upper arm. "But I shall."

"But Husband—" The words choked.

Dan shook her. "You will allow Lady Esmeralda to examine my babe. If you make one sound or twist your face up in any contorted fashion, so help me…" He waved Esmeralda forward.

With trembling hands, she ran them over the bulge in Olva's middle. Closing her eyes, and with light pressure, she found the babe's head to determine its position and general size. The little life pressed a foot against her hand as she continued to explore.

"Is everything to right?" Dan's words were tight.

Esmeralda smiled. "All seems well with the babe."

"And Olva?" He sounded less concerned about his wife.

"I would like to check one other thing."

Dan nodded.

She looked between the couple for a moment—unsure.

"Do whatever you think best, and don't worry. I know my wife well."

Olva huffed and squirmed, but didn't dare refuse as Dan still had a grip on her arm.

Esmeralda nodded and completed her exam with haste. "Olva's body does not seem at all prepared to deliver which is good. I believe whatever triggered the labor pains is gone and not likely to return. She may continue with her normal activities at once." Turning to Olva, she added. "Go slow in the beginning. Don't over tax yourself until you know for sure the pains will not begin again."

"Thank you, m'lady." Dan inclined his head, and she slipped outside with Newt.

A short time later, Esz arrived in the communal hall but only a handful of men were there. She found Jeni, Heart, and Kel in the kitchen. "Where is everyone?"

Jeni offered a quick smile. "Out defending king and country as I understand it. They dashed out of here this morning in full armor talking of an uprising somewhere."

"It happens now and then," Kel offered taking a tray out.

"We feed the few left here to watch over us. Some in the hall, while for those stationed on the wall we deliver the food to them." Heart filled four baskets and handed her two. "Shall we?"

Once everyone had eaten, no matter where they were, Esmeralda sat with the women. It seemed ridiculous to eat at the high table alone. She noted the raised brows and knew Tiobald would again give the *proper place* speech, but for the moment, she didn't care. She also noted that all the husbands had remained behind. All except hers.

Tiobald and the others did not return by the next morning. A group gathered for the hunt. She watched Newt eye the men. "You should join them."

"M'lady?"

"There are few hands for the hunt with all the others gone. You should join them and help."

"But m'lord gave instructions—"

"Truly, Newt, I have herbs to tend, Olva to look in on, and little more. Jeni hopes to teach me more cooking if time allows. Go hunt. I shall be more than fine."

His head swiveled from her to the group mounting and back again.

"Go," she insisted and walked off to the chapel.

Returning after Jeni and she received the Word from Brother Joanis, movement at the gate caught her eye. A horse returned with a man slumped in the saddle. Esmeralda ran to him. She remembered bringing him food yesterday, but did not recall his name. Blood oozed from his leg. No one was around. Even those on the wall were too far to yell for.

The man moaned.

"I'll help you. Where do you live?"

He pointed and she led the horse down the same lane as Tiobald's home and several homes beyond. She pulled him from the horse and dragged him inside.

Chapter 30

Tio rode back through the shire gates as the sun disappeared beyond the horizon. He both longed to see Esmeralda and dreaded it. They were at odds, and it was his fault. Newt took his mount as he approached his home.

"How is Esmeralda?"

"I don't know, m'lord."

"What do you mean? Why not?"

"She sent me out to hunt this morning. With so few of us, it took longer than usual and the drove, led by the brute we've tried numerous times to corner, is becoming more troublesome. We prepared a stag we'd brought down when he, and his growing assortment of sows, rampaged our group, scattered the horses, and sent men running men into trees. We only just now returned. I haven't seen your lady as yet. I knocked, but she doesn't seem to be within."

Tio's fists clenched and unclenched and Newt took a step back. "You were supposed to watch her." The words ground slowly through his locked jaw.

"But, sir—"

Movement farther down the lane caught Tio's attention. Esmeralda. She staggered out of Otger's home. Rage tore open his chest. Burned his skin. And blurred his vision.

"ESMERALDA!"

She jumped at his bellow, and cringed from him as he stormed toward her. Her gown, hands, and arms were covered in blood. "I tried. Truly, I did." Her head shook and her entire body quaked. "Time. We needed more time."

He seized her by the arms and jerked her out of her ramblings. "What have you done?"

She whimpered and coward from him. "I tried."

Newt returned from inside Otger's home. "He's dead, m'lord. That boar tore up his leg something awful. I don't know how he even made it back here."

"I found him slumped on his horse at the gate. He remained awake long enough to point to his home."

"And you took him there? Inside his home? Alone? In front of everyone, you flaunted your wanton behavior?"

Her head snapped up. Eyes wide at first, then they narrowed on him. She slammed her hands into his chest forcing him back a step. "How dare you! There was no one here when he returned. No one to help me, and no one to *see* me."

"So, you were sneaking around—"

Again, her hands smashed against his chest and drove him back another step. "I was trying to save his life! How much do you hate me that you would bellow to the entire shire that I am wanton when the man was nearly dead when I found him? Do you think me vile enough to try and lie with a dying man only doors away from your home?" Her voice caught and her eyes filled with pools. "Do you think me shameful enough I would so quickly throw off the vows I took before my God and do something so utterly unthinkable?"

Ice filled his veins. He froze as he witnessed her pain and hatred. She would never do what he'd accused her of. His eyes took in those standing at a distance but clearly taking notice.

Esmeralda stifled a cry and ran from him. His legs quaked trying to keep him upright. Every day he only made things worse between them.

But this… this was unforgivable.

"Otger is dead." Tio slouched in a chair in Dunlang's home.

"Aye, I heard."

Tio considered his hands as they dangled off his knees. "Then you know?"

"That you accused that wonderful woman who has done nothing but good for this town of being a harlot with a man taking his last breath? Oh, aye. I am more than aware."

"What is the matter with me?"

Dunlang stood and put his hand on Tio's shoulder. "I have done you no favors."

Tio glanced at him.

"I came here to save our family. Then I lost my children one by one, followed soon by my wife, then my sister. I continued to hide in the shadow of fear I cast over all of us. You came by that fear easily enough. I have been a right poor example, and for that, I am sore sorry."

"I have done a fair job of mucking everything up on my own."

"Oh, that you have." Dunlang thumped him on the back before returning to his chair and his tankard. "Your fear is driving her away, Tio. You can ill afford to lose her. I see how she stirs you. You'll never find another, and if you should choose to put her aside, our enemies would use it against you to further challenge your rule. Short of her death, you cannot refuse her now that you have chosen."

Tio rubbed his head. "There is so much weighing on me—on our future, I don't know where to being."

Dunlang leaned forward, and raised his tankard to his Second. "First you must convince your bride that she still is, in fact, your wife."

Chapter 31

"Esmeralda?" Tio tapped on the middle door. Her sniffles quieted and the door flew open. A blood-covered mass of fabric lay in a heap by the sputtering fire. She was dressed in a clean gown, though it was well into the night.

"Are you escorting me out of Rustshade?" Her words were curt and her gaze was hard.

"Escorting you out?"

"Are you finally done with me? Ready to throw me out like a rotting carcass?" Her voice betrayed her, and she buried her face in her hands.

Tio dropped to a chair. "Oh, Esmeralda. I want nothing of the kind. You are my wife—"

She stomped her foot. "Stop saying that!" She whirled to re-enter her room, and he snatched her hand, then pulled her close.

Taking up her other hand also, he lowered to the chair. He laid his forehead against the back of her hands and held her firm as she tried to pull free. "And you must stop saying such. You are my wife, and I have been a fool."

"You called me wanton." Her choked whisper tore open his heart.

"'Twas a horrible mistake. This is not the world you came from, Esmeralda. Our men have long been without the warmth and comfort of a woman. You tempt them."

She tried to jerk free. "I do not. I am not flitting about town trying to entice any man to my bed."

He shook his head against her hands. "Not with intention, nay. But you know no boundary. You go anywhere without thought for what you put our men through. You are the most desirable woman ever to come to our shire."

"To all but the one who matters it would seem." Her mutter was so low he nearly missed it.

His head rose, and he kissed her hands. "Esmeralda—"

A knock on the door stopped him. Newt called out, "M'lord, Lord Dunlang prepares to ride out again with the men. There has been a sighting of the Force of Echoes."

He didn't want to leave. There was so much he needed to tell her.

She pulled from his hands, then turned away. "Go. You don't want to be here anyway."

He leapt up, snatched her arm, and spun her. His hand cradled her cheek. His forehead pressed to hers. "Our enemies are too close. I go only to keep you safe. For our future. There will be one, if you don't give up on me." Her mouth opened, but he placed his finger to her lips. "Please, swear to me you will be here when I return, and will still be mine." She tried to pull away again.

"M'lord?" Newt called again.

"Saddle my horse. I'm coming." Frustration soured his tone. A slow breath eased from him. He held Esmeralda tighter and tangled his fingers into her hair. "Please, promise me."

"I don't understand you."

"I know. But will you promise?"

"I will be here."

He kissed her forehead and left before temptation overtook him and he fulfilled his vow with her and threw off his duty to his people.

The days shortened and cooled. Tio did not return for over a week as other matters far more important than she consumed his time. She pulled the warm wheat bread from one of the common ovens in the center of town, and set the golden mound to cool, then stood with her eyes closed for a moment. *Lord, I go again to face the hatred of Olva. My guilt and shame overwhelm me. Coupled with her hatred and Tiobald's indifference, this is too much for me to bear. Help me, please, Lord.*

She had avoided the distasteful visit as long as she could. Mayhaps she should visit the chapel again. She released the breath held tight within her. Best to face it and be done.

"Good day to you, sir." She greeted Dan as he stepped outside and ushered her within.

"Good day, m'lady." As always, he left her alone.

"Check and see that my babe and I are fine and be gone." Olva said under her breath.

Esmeralda knelt beside Olva as she sat at her meal table. Dirty dishes scattered around her and stacked on the cutboard. A rat scurried into a dark hole with a bit of dry bread.

"Don't wrinkle your nose at me, wench. I can't see to my duties as a good wife while you worry my husband over the life of his child. We are both fine." Her hand caressed her belly. "My son and I would be better without your constant interference."

"Nay have I put any restrictions on your activities, as well you know. And your daughter is hale and still due to arrive in two months."

"Daughter? You don't think I can give my husband a son?"

Esmeralda shrugged as her hands slid over Olva's stomach. She noted the babe's activity, and position. "I am sure both of you are capable of producing a son. But such things are in the hand of God, and I think your child be a girl."

Olva burst from the chair, upsetting Esmeralda's balance making her plop on her rear. "Get out. And don't return."

Brushing herself off, Esmeralda moved to the door. "That, as always, will depend on your husband's wishes."

A ray of weak sunlight splashed over her, and she paused for a moment. She had survived another encounter and had not been brought to tears. She coughed twice as a breeze chilled her.

"Does all proceed as it ought?" Dan stood wringing his hands.

"Yes. They are both well and there are no signs the pains have returned."

"Does she treat you kindly and appreciate your care?" It was the same question Dan asked every time she came.

She gave her same response. "Olva and I are getting on."

Dan stared at her, not allowing his gaze to release her. "A daughter?"

He'd heard? But how much?

"Aye, I know the ills of my wife. I know she treats you horribly. Yet you will not speak of it."

"As I have said, what is between us occurred long ago and cannot be mended by my insignificant acts here."

"Still you shield her and take the brunt of her anger without retaliation."

"I wish her only health and joy, sir, as I do you."

His smile grew to fill his round face. "A daughter. To bounce on my knee and swing through the air. A grand thing indeed. But there will be hard days ahead to see she does not become her sharp-tongued mother."

"Dan!" Olva stood in the doorway.

"Don't think you might scold me, Wife. Your tongue has the bite of a viper, and I have a mind to cut it from your head. Now, as m'lady has said, you suffer no restrictions, though you fain weakness at every opportunity. I go to gather wood. The house *will* be clean by the time I return. Or you *will* regret it."

Olva shielded her middle. "You would not dare strike me while I carry your child."

"Nay, I would not. But remember, in two months I will hold that babe in my arms, and your life will be mine to do with as I see fit. Prove to me you will be a good wife and mother and I may change my mind and not send you away."

"You," she pointed a finger at Esmeralda. "This is your fault. If you can't kill my family, you poison their minds against me."

Dan grabbed Olva's arm and pushed her inside the house. "Forgive us, m'lady. Your presence will not be required until my daughter chooses to present herself. I'll not have you subjected to Olva's hatred any longer. Good day, m'lady." The door closed on all but Olva's tears.

Esmeralda lumbered back to collect her bread and return to Tiobald's house, with Newt, as always, in her wake.

A man waited at her door. Grey hair hiding his eyes and bent with age, but still he managed to bow low. "M'lady."

"Hubert, how might I aid you?"

"I didn't wish to bother ya 'bout such a lit'le thin', but…" He held out his hand. One digit was twice the size of those beside it.

"Looks to be infected. Come inside and—"

"No, ma'am. I couldn't." He sputtered. Newt stood beside him with arms crossed. A disapproving scowl marring his fine face.

"Oh, you men. Honestly." She stomped inside, tossed the bread at the cutboard and pitched a chair out the open door. Followed quickly by another.

"M'lady what—?"

She dropped the unread scrolls on the floor and dragged the table to the door. It was hard to wedge it through the narrow opening. "As I can't stand to drain and tend the wound and Hubert can't be expected to hold still standing either, and you are both too bull-headed to come inside where this might be done properly, it is left to me—again—to see that the matter might be accomplished."

"Here, let me help," Newt said.

Esmeralda released the table as she coughed several times.

Newt stared at her; the table held in his hands. She pointed as the coughing continued.

After rinsing her hands with water from the pitcher inside, she sat across from Hubert.

"Sorry of all the trouble, m'lady."

"Would have been easier and warmer inside, but as that seems against some law, this will have to do." She coughed intermittently as she drained the ragged gash of any signs of infection, slathered it in her cream to ward off its return, and wrapped it in a bit of clean cloth. She put some of the balm in another jar and handed it to Hubert with several more fabric strips. "Clean it with fresh water, reapply the ointment, and rewrap it in a new cloth twice a day." She stood with a smile. "If it doesn't improve in two days, come back and see me."

Hubert bowed his bent frame. "What do I owe ya, m'lady?"

She waved off the gesture. "Lord Tiobald provides all I need."

"I can't take this from ya without pay."

"It is truly my great honor to be of aid. I require nothing."

Tio returned to find Esmeralda sitting outside their home holding another man's hand. Sure, it was only old Hubert, and she was attentively treating an injury, but how the sight made him rage—bringing to mind the sight of her leaving Otger's home. Though part of his brain screamed for him to stop and think, he couldn't control himself. He hated to see her with other men. He stomped up, fists clenched tight, muscles aching from their constriction only to catch her words. Soft and gentle, and spoken without guile. She'd said he provided all she needed. Mayhaps his last actions had not deepened her rejection of him.

She turned to re-enter the house and almost collided with him. "Tio." She broke off in a fit of coughing.

Tio worked to release the tension still holding him captive as Hubert bowed and acknowledged him.

"Yar lady wife will not accept payment for her time and healin' items, m'lord."

"Esmeralda is a woman with a generous heart. If she says she requires no payment, then go with God, and may you be soon healed, Hubert." Tio never took his eyes off Esmeralda.

"Thank ya, m'lord, m'lady."

"Good eve to you Hubert. Come see me again if you need more." Esmeralda shivered and coughed again.

"Are you hale?"

She nodded slipping past him inside. She warmed herself by the fire. "Sitting out in the cold did me no favors."

"But you couldn't entertain him inside." He brought back in one of the chairs they had used.

"Leave them out there. People are already afraid to seek me out after your last outburst. If I'm burdened moving them every time they have need of me, they will never come. And," she perched hands on her hips. Did she look even thinner? "I was not *entertaining* the man. I was treating his injury." She coughed several times again.

Tio stepped close, his gaze searching her face. "You don't sound at all good, Esz."

She waved him off. "I'll make a tea with horehound and be fine."

"You should retire. Rest. I can make the stew for tonight."

"Oh, stop fussing. What difference would it make anyway? It's not as if you'd miss me."

He seized her and spun her around, then gripped her upper arms. "Never say that again!"

She startled in his grasp and he softened. Leaning forward until his forehead rested against hers, he whispered. "I would *not* survive if anything happened to Esz. Truly I wouldn't."

She drew back; her face scrunched in confusion. "I do not

understand you, m'lord." When he didn't say more, she pulled entirely from his hold and started chopping vegetables adding them to the pot over the fire.

She had been warm in his hands. Her forehead smooth as silk against his. It took every ounce of his strength not to draw her into his arms and kiss her soundly. But the memory of he screams of the women who had been part of his life before her, echoed in his skull driving out the fire.

Chapter 32

Esmeralda woke with a start. The door to her bedchamber stood open. She watched the confusing man bustling about in the living chamber. He was more than protective, outright jealous at times, but when they were alone, he acted as though he would be infected if he touched her. Even now, he turned away to avoid looking at her in her chemise.

She pulled a gown over her head and stepped into the outer room. "If seeing me is so unpleasant, then leave the door closed."

"'Tis too cold for you. Will only exasperate the cough. Would be far better to be in the main bedchamber."

"When you see fit to join me…" she let the words hang between them.

His muscles strained against his tunic, but he didn't turn to look at her. "You should rest today."

"'Tis the Lord's Day. I go to service."

Tio put out his hand to stop her. "At least make some tea for your cough before we go."

"But the sacraments?"

At last he turned. The deep furrow between his brows and the tenderness in his eyes pulled her to a stop. "The good Lord would not fault you for treating a cough so that you might sit at peace to hear more of Him." When she didn't move, Tio waved out a hand toward the fire. "Please. The water is hot."

Esmeralda put in a fair amount of honey before gathering her satchel of herbs and adding them to the cup. Tio ladled water into it and sat with her at the table. His stare searched her. For several moments, she sipped the soothing brew letting the sweet honey and warmth coat her stinging throat.

"I don't wish you to sit out in the cold and treat the injured and sick."

She plunked the cup down with a *thunk*. "You don't want me to go in any man's home. You don't want any other man in your home. Now you don't want me to treat anyone outside. Am I Rustshade's healer or not?"

He cradled his head in his hands. "I think only of you, Esmeralda. Of your health and your reputation."

"I may have had the reputation of a witch in Flatwell, but no one dared call me a whore." She stood, leaving the empty cup, and moved to the door. "They knew a healer had to go to where the sick are be them men or women, in their homes, in the tavern, or in the inn."

Outside, the sun was not high enough or strong enough to penetrate through the naked trees. She shivered.

Tio wrapped a short cloak around her. His hand lingered on her shoulders and slid down her arms in a gentle caress. "I do not think you a fallen woman."

"Then why—?"

He put up his hand to stay her. His hands gripped her arms again, and he pressed his forehead to hers. "As I have said, the men here sore miss their womenfolk. And I could not bear it, if anyone thought less of you."

She wanted to stay in his half-embrace. It was the most she could expect from him. But the chapel bell beckoned. "Then mayhaps you need to instruct your people of my duties and what is required of me."

She jerked from his grasp to avoid coughing in his face. Why didn't the tea work? A shuddered skipped across her shoulders.

"Come, let's get you out of the cold." He walked closer than normal as they moved to the chapel. When they sat, he moved so close they touched.

Esmeralda still struggled with the notion that men and women sat together here. Unlike Flatwell, the aisle didn't divide them. She normally found Tio's distance from her distracting. But at the moment it was his nearness that almost kept Brother Joanis' words from reaching her thoughts.

"You should return home and rest," he said as they stepped outside after the service.

"You are constantly pestering me about eating, and now you want me to skip a meal?"

"I'll bring you plenty. But there is no need to go and extend yourself when you are ill."

She started walking to the common building. "It is a cough, nothing more. And how would it look if the healer was taking to bed at the least little thing?"

Tio drew alongside her, shoulders sagging, head low. "At least don't serve today."

"I am no glass jar that will break so easily."

"Nay, Esz, you are strong enough for the both of us."

She stumbled to a stop and stared at him. What did that mean?

"Esz." Jeni engulfed her in a hug, snatched up her hand, and dragged her to the kitchens. Due to being captured by her friend, Esmeralda couldn't question Tio. Pulled into a dark corner while the other women sliced meat and chesses and filled trays, Jeni held Esmeralda still. "It's happened."

"What?"

"I'm with child." She nearly bounced up and down.

Esmeralda hugged her to hide the disappointment she feared would show on her own face. She was to help a town of women bring forth new life but never know the joy herself. Her cough returned making her break the hold.

"Esz, are you well?"

"Just a little tickle, brought to life by your good news. The Lord bless you."

"It's all because of you—"

"You two going to help or gossip in the corner like little girls?" The bite of Olva's tongue sobered them both, and they moved toward the others.

After the tables were served, she sat at her place to Tio's right. Still, he provided no better companionship than when she dined with Dunlang alone. Tio watched her like a hawk soaring over a field of mice.

Her cough calmed and she ate what her nervous stomach would allow. Would she ever find peace with this confounding man? But she wanted more than peace. She needed to love and be loved. She needed it most desperately.

Chapter 33

Tio cleared his throat to address the council. "I have a concern I must bring before you. Esmeralda has taken it upon herself to serve our community as healer."

"And blessed we are for it," Wilm shouted.

"Aye, she has lifted the stink of curse and left hope," Dunlang added. "But tell us, Tio, how does this concern you?"

"Though not well respected in her own town, she still moved about freely and treated all who would allow be them women or men. She has been quite bold to tell me, in Flatwell, she treated more than one man alone in his home. She has attempted to do the same here. Newt has tried to watch over her and guide her in our laws in an effort to keep her from appearing brazen. We know who she is and what she will mean to all our people. But I fear my restrictions on her have begun to cause her harm. She has developed a cough. Two eves past, she sat outside in the cold to treat old Hubert's infected finger. As the winter deepens, she will be more and more inclined to treat out of doors because of our protection over our women. I am, however, at a loss as to what to do."

Muttered agreement hummed in the room as the men bent their heads together.

"We can't afford a double standard for her that is not permitted for the other women. She, above the others, must set an example for all those she is to lead."

"It would lead to resentment as well," another man added.

"True, but we can nay put our blessed healer at risk or forbade her to treat the men."

"She needs someone to accompany her."

The buzz in the room rose to that of an agreeable beehive.

"Who do you suggest?"

"Has to be one of the women."

Zeke stood. "Will be my Jeni." All discussion ceased. "Jeni adores Lady Esmeralda. A long-lost sister, she has called her. They've already worked Lady Esmeralda's herbs into Jeni's garden, and Jeni has been a comfort to our lady."

There was nodded agreement around the room. "Thank you, Zeke. Ask Jeni if she would be agreeable. It is not an order," Tio said.

Zeke released a guffaw as he sat. "You shall hear the shriek of delight as soon as I return home. I assure you."

The meeting concluded with other business quickly addressed, though Tio paid little attention. How would Esz view this new arrangement? Would she see Jeni as a nursemaid as she did Newt? Or would she feel freer to do what she loved?

Before he had time to broach the issue with her, a wagon came barreling through the gate. "M'lord," Connin shouted reigning in. "We need your lady wife."

"No, we don't," a voice groaned from the wagon bed.

"I'm here." Esmeralda rushed past Tio; her hem held high—too high.

Garrett struggled to lower himself to the ground. Blood made his trouser leg cling to the skin. He teetered on two makeshift crutches. "Nay, m'lady. I'll be right in not time. No need to trouble you."

"'Tis no trouble, but 'tis more serious then you believe."

"I'll go home and rest."

Esmeralda's hands went to her hips. Never a good sign. Tio braced himself for what she would say or do next.

"Very well. Your lord and lady would be pleased to dine with you this night." She came along side Garrett, her steps firm and purposeful. Tio stayed close at her heels.

Garrett struggled to his home, pushed open the door, and she followed him inside.

She plopped into a chair and rubbed her arms. "Your fire seems to have gone out, Garrett. Your lady is cold."

"I'll help—" she raised her hand and glared at Tio, cutting his words short.

"The Lord Sheriff and Second of all Rustshade cannot be expected to build the fire as a guest in another man's home." Her tone indignant, Tio stared at her. She'd never leaned on his title before. Didn't seem to care for it at most times. Had she been spending too much time with Olva?

Garrett hobbled around, trying to carry some kindling to the hearth while maneuvering on the crutches or hopping on his good leg.

Esmeralda's teeth shattered. Was she truly so cold?

When he nearly dropped a small log on Tio's foot, Garrett groaned. "M'lady, mayhaps another day might be better."

"Unless you allow me to treat your wound now, you will never again have use of that leg. Should you survive the infection I can already smell festering, you will require aids to walk for the rest of your life. Never will you be able to carry things in your arms as you have always done."

"Esmeralda," Tio tried to soften her.

She sprang to her feet. "I speak the truth. Garrett is still a young man. Now that the concerns weighing on Rustshade have been lifted, he could seek a new wife. Have children. But none will be possible if he dies or is left maimed."

Garrett sagged into a chair as a groan escaped through his clenched teeth. "As you will, m'lady."

"Very good. Remove your trousers."

"What?"

"Esmeralda," Tio's shout echoed through the room.

"Oh, goose feathers to the highest heavens. Men. Honestly." She pointed at Tio. "Take him to his bed and assist him. I have items to gather."

"But, Esmer—"

She was through the door. "Best to cut the pant leg free to prevent worsening the injury," she called.

Tio and Garrett stared at one another.

"M'lord, I'm not inclined to be bare before your lady wife."

"Neither am I." Tio worked to unclench his fists. "But better remove your clothing and cover yourself well before she returns. I have no doubt she'll do it herself if we do not comply."

They both gulped, and Tio shook off his irritation as he helped the man into his bed. Jeni wouldn't be able to help with this. How was he to make this work?

Chapter 34

Esmeralda stuffed down her ire, took a slow measured breath, and in her most gentile tone, called out from the doorway. "Am I allowed to enter?"

"Come." Tio ground the word out. He stood beside Garrett's bed, his arms crossed but fists so tight they had lost all color. This was going to be a long evening.

Garrett's left leg lay exposed below the knee—it rested at an odd angel. The rest of him was well covered.

Esmeralda dropped the items she'd brought and knelt beside the bed. She exposed the slightest amount of his hip. Tio growled and Garrett tensed. Esmeralda swallowed her exasperation. "Relax. It will pain you less." She pressed and felt. Tio glowered with such heat, she was sure someone had lit the fire.

"I must touch him." She stood. "As must you." She pointed for Tio to move behind Garrett. "The blood has slowed, I will tend to this first."

Esmeralda's hands roamed freely over Garrett's exposed flesh. This was completely unacceptable. Tio wanted to throw her over his shoulder and march her home. But she spoke truth—as always. If the injury wasn't treated, Garrett would never walk again.

She coughed against her arm before she could direct him. "Sit behind him and wrap an arm around his stomach. Hold him still and provide me tension to work against."

As Tio moved into place, Esmeralda placed one knee between Garrett's legs and wrapped her slight hands round his leg above the knee.

Tio couldn't see as the world blurred in a red haze. Pressure built in his skull pitching his stomach, which was in a knot unlike any he ever experienced. Her hands should never be on another man and never like this.

She smiled at Garrett. She'd never smiled at him like that. "Garrett, tell me, when you are well mended, what kind of woman will you be looking for?"

"I don't know, m'lady."

"Tall, short?" She coughed twice.

"Not too much of either, I suppose."

"Light hair, dark hair?"

Garrett shrugged.

More coughing. "Tell me you don't wish a red head."

Garrett chuckled.

"We redheads are said to be ill-tempered and hard to deal with. Speak our mind."

"Oh m'lady, you are gentile and a right proper lady."

"Even with how I've treated you today?" She shied away with a bit of a giggle. "You know some say the fire in a person's soul is what ignites the hair."

"A fiery soul can't be all bad."

She tipped her head away to cough, then she held his gaze. She pulled and twisted and the leg popped back into place in his hip.

Air whistled through Garrett's teeth. "You tricked me, m'lady." The air strained through the man.

She lifted from the bed and went back to examine the hip. "Was easier to accomplish when you were relaxed. You won't like what I do next either." She slipped her hand under his knee and lifted it working the hip.

Tio stood as Garrett winced against the pain.

"Good. That works as it ought." She coughed as she went to the supplies she'd brought and picked up a long strip of cloth. "Now we'll secure the hip with this." She reached for the sheet to fully uncover him.

Tio seized her hand, and Garrett grasped the sheet stopping her.

She thrust the fabric at Tio. "Goose feathers." She walked to the end of the bed and turned her back, arms crossed. "Half the length is to go under him."

Tio followed each of her instructions until the sling was in place.

Esmeralda shifted her attention to the lower part of Garrett's leg. Dried blood hid the extent of the injury. As she turned to collect more of her supplies, she coughed before she touched Tio on the forearm. "I'll need a fire, if you would."

Tio brought the flame to life and soon a pot of water simmered over it. She continued to cough as she heated a slender blade in it. Long after the sun slipped into its slumber, Esmeralda worked to clean the cut and cauterized it. She set the bone, bound the leg with a splint, sutured the wound, and dressed the injury with her herbs. She worked tirelessly while talking with Garrett. Her quiet banter was only interrupted by her frequent coughing, yet served to calm both men. Tio had to admit she was a wonder.

Garrett's leg well-tended, Esmeralda made him a tea. "Now, you'll need someone to stay with you for a few days."

"I'll ask Connin," Tio said.

"He has duties on the wall, m'lord."

Esmeralda looked to Tio. "It will only be for a few days, until the leg is sure not to slip from the hip again."

Tio nodded. "Connin can be spared from his other responsibilities for that time."

She turned back to Garrett. "After, you should be able to manage on the crutches until the break is set. You are to put no weight on the leg for a couple fortnights, mayhaps more. I'll check on the wound to make sure it does not sicken." Esmeralda coughed as she collected her items. "The tea will ease the pain and help with sleep. But I'll bring some stew later."

"You have done more than enough, m'lady."

She smiled at him as Tio held open the door for her. "I am pleased I could be of some aid. Rest. I'll return later."

They walked out into the night, but her coughing consumed his attention. "Newt will deliver the meal." He waved the young man over, instructed him to have Connin come to Garrett's home as soon as possible, then come to their home and wait for the stew Tio would prepare.

"Am I never to be allowed to do my assigned task?" Her words were quiet—defeated.

"I spoke with the council today, and it was agreed upon that Jeni would assist you in order to maintain your honor. But it would have been unseemly for either of you, or both of you, to undress Garrett. I am at a loss as how to allow the shire access to your healing without compromising your reputation."

"Newt can assist, as you did, this night."

Tio stopped. The idea had merit. "I will think on it."

"Esz!" Jeni bound up to her friend. "M'lord," she acknowledged him with a quick incline of her head before turning back to Esmeralda. She looped her arm with his wife's and they strolled away. "Zeke says I am to work with you. Where do we begin?"

Esmeralda coughed, then tipped her head so it rested against Jeni's. "In the morn, my friend. Garrett suffered a serious injury. We will visit him."

"What of Olva?"

Esmeralda's feet dragged. "Dan has said I don't need to return every day, but I suppose I should check on her. I would never forgive myself…"

"Thank you, Jeni, for your kindness to Esmeralda. She'll see you in the morning." Tio pushed open the door to their home. The women spoke their parting as Esmeralda came inside.

"You didn't need to usher her away so soon."

"I have ears, Esz. Your cough worsens."

She nodded and hung a pot of water beside the stew pot. As they waited for the meal to cook, Tio sat with her at the table. "Will you tell me of what happened with Olva?"

She looked up through long lashes, her gaze searching him.

"I don't believe you killed her mother, but there is something that happened for you to cower so under her wrath."

She wrung her hands and stared at the table. "But I am to blame none-the-less."

Chapter 35

Tio had asked, as she feared he would. He needed to know the manner of woman she was, but she knew it would only drive them further apart. She pushed to her feet and idly stirred the stew.

"Olva's mum had an even sharper tongue than her daughter's."

"Ooh." Tio's chair scraped against the floor as he shifted.

"She said such vile, hateful things about MeeMa. Turned the entire town against her. After her tirade, no one dared openly seek out the gentle healer or me when they were in need." She watched the swirl and ripples she created while she stirred.

"But then she fell ill." Tio's tenderness prodded her to continue.

"I knew Mary was sick. MeeMa and I both offered to help, but our aid was harshly rebuffed."

"Then there is no blame for you."

She shook her head. "I should have tried harder. But I wished ill on the woman. I wanted God to make Mary suffer as she had done to MeeMa. It was ungodly of me. We are to care for our enemies not wish terrible things to befall them. I should have done more. But I refused to go and try to help until Olva pleaded with me. By then, 'twas too late."

Tio's hand rested high on her back, warm, reassuring. "This is why you will not relent now when you see a need. Why you spoke so to Garrett."

She looked up at him. "I can't live with allowing another to suffer by my inaction." He was so close. She wanted—needed—his arms to wrap around her. To hold her tight and tell her she wouldn't burn in hell for the way she'd treated Olva's mum.

But Tio moved away, picked up the smallest of their pots and ladled stew into it. "You bear no blame, Esz. The woman made her decision. And no one faults you for what you did, or didn't do."

"Olva does. And God judges the heart."

"God sees how you care for each life entrusted to you." He pushed through the door and handed the pot to Newt. He turned to look at her again. "I did not see you treat Kel, but I watched you this eve and you are—" His next words whispered with awe. "You are blessed by God Himself."

He did not condemn her, but neither did his touch comfort her. Whatever barrier lay between them was no worse but neither was it better. They ate in near silence other than her continuing cough and she soon turned to her bed.

"You have labored hard. Rest you well, Eszy."

She stared at him. A flutter dancing around her heart.

"Do you wish I not call you that?"

She shook her head. "MeeMa was the only one to ever call me Eszy, other than Mum." She fought as the tears of their loss pooled afresh. "It feels like home."

He stood before her, less than an arm-length away. "Welcome home, Eszy."

The need to be held overwhelmed her and she stepped forward. But he stepped back. "Rest you well." He turned and left the house. She shivered in his absence as a new fit of coughing struck her. Hugging her arms tight about her, she buried herself under the covers; that it was dirt covering her in death and not mere fabric.

Tio fled into the cold night like the coward his was. She needed him, but he couldn't respond. He wouldn't allow himself her touch. He couldn't resist her if he dared. The need in her eyes, the longing of his own flesh, and the desire in his heart, tore at him. The entire community needed her. More than he. He tried to convince himself he did the right thing, but he knew it was fear alone that propelled him.

The night cooled his fire and he set his ax to logs to relieve the tension. Nothing though, could drive out the memory of the hurt in her eyes. Best for him to return to nearby Haven or another battle break out with their enemy and spare that lovely creature any more of the pain he inflected. When he returned home, he added wood to the flames to drive out any chill from the house and determined to leave at first light.

Tio's eyes fell on her covered form in the flickering light. She drew him like a thirsty deer to a gentle stream. In that moment, he knew he wouldn't be able to stay away.

Chapter 36

"Eszy?" Tiobald whispered into her dreams. He sounded of home and comfort. His word quiet and gentle. Yet he did not want her. "Eszy?"

"Yes, m'lord." She raised her head and the cough returned.

"Rest this day. Heal. I must leave on a matter of some import. I may again be gone a day or two." He started to turn. "Take Jeni and Newt with you when you are well enough to leave."

She dropped back to her pillow. "As you wish." The outer door latched. Clearly the man cared for her. He worried over what his people thought of her. Wished her to be hale. Praised all she did—even her terrible cooking. Yet, he would not draw near her. Rarely did he dare touch her. Mayhaps he *did* suffer some lack. Something that prevented him coming to their marriage bed.

Esmeralda pushed to her feet, tossed a gown over her head, threw a clean one over her arm, gathered up a basket in the corner of her room, and stepped outside.

"Good morn to you, m'lady," Newt said with a yawn.

"Good morn. You need not accompany me at the moment. I but go to bathe. I will collect Jeni and then find you before going to Garrett."

"As you wish m'lady." He escorted her to the common bath building nonetheless.

She filled the large bronze tub with heated water and added her own collection of oils and flowers. The room filled with the aroma of lavender and rose. She slipped in, letting the warmth cover her completely. When she surfaced with a gasp a few moments later Jeni knelt beside her. Arms crossed on the side of the tub, chin resting on top, she grinned like a child up to mischief.

"I've never seen anyone who can hold their breath as long as you."

Esmeralda leaned her head back and closed her eyes. "I treasure the silence and the escape beneath the surface."

"What could you possibly have to escape?" Jeni flitted about the room. She added more wood to the hearth where the water heated, and splashed more oils in bath.

"Please don't be so liberal. It will be months before the flowers bloom again."

"Oh, don't be such a curmudgeon." She sat beside the tub again. "What has you in such a mood?"

"I'm not in a mood."

"Oh, don't fret, Esz. It will happen to you as well."

"Happen?"

"You have done so much save us; God is sure to bless you with a child soon." Jeni's hand gripped Esz's shoulder.

Esmeralda let her head drop back again. There would be no children in her future. Sooner or later everyone in the shire would know that either they had never come together or that one of them was damaged. Not something either of them wanted to face.

"Come now. Finish your cleaning. No time to wallow."

Esmeralda's cough resurfaced as she dried and dressed causing Jeni to consider her. "I'm fine," Esz protested, but the persistent irritant was beginning to concern her too.

Soon they walked arm in arm and headed toward Garrett's home. It was hard to be morose in Jeni's presence. She bubbled joy. Esmeralda was soon laughing.

Jeni became her anchor over the next weeks. She saw little of

Tiobald, choosing instead to put as much distance between them as possible. Garrett's healing proceeded without concern. Esmeralda and Jeni spent much of their time in Tiobald's home, grinding the herbs that had dried and arranging them in jars on shelves she added to the wall.

At first, Tio returned every couple of nights, then only on the Lord's Day. Several times, the majority of men left dressed for battle. When they returned, she would tend to wounds or broken bones. Tio was not always with them.

A large band of men had flown out the gate in the morn. Esmeralda insisted Newt join them. She and Jeni worked quietly with no injured to attend when a light knock came to her door.

Kel stuck her head inside. "'Tis Olva. The babe comes."

They brushed their hands clean and moved to the door. Jeni gathered the satchel with the herbs. They both donned their aprons and forearm coverings and hurried through the town.

Dan paced outside. He huffed a breath slowly. "Good, you're here."

Jeni and Kel went inside but she lingered for a moment. "Bringing forth a child is difficult and can be long even at its best. I'll not go into the bedchamber unless I'm needed. Would only add to Olva's discomfort. I'll pray I'm not needed."

"But you'll go?"

"If necessary. I'll do all I can to help them both." Esmeralda moved to kneel before the hearth in the living chamber. Over the sounds of Olva's labor, she prayed.

Her legs lost all feeling as the time past. But there were no screams. No distress beyond what any woman experienced.

"M'lady!" Kel shouted.

Esmeralda popped to her feet, stumbled on tingling legs, and hastened into the room.

"What? What's the matter? No. Not her, no." Olva strained against the hands holding her.

Moving to Kel where she sat guiding the babe, Esmeralda ignored Olva's protest of her presence.

"Don't let her touch my babe. She'll kill it."

The child's face was deeper red than it should have been almost verging on purple. The babe's lips a sickly blue. Esmeralda shouldered Kel aside as she knelt at the birthing stool. "Is a knife prepared?" She asked Kel.

"Aye, m'lady."

"Bring it and prepare to tie off the cord."

"What are you doing?" Olva screeched.

"Bear down, Olva." The sharp order silenced the woman, and she strained to bring the babe forth. Hastening the shoulders through with a twist, Esmeralda cut the cord wrapped around the babe's throat.

The flash of the blade drew a shriek from Olva who thrashed about. "No! Don't kill him."

"Hush, Olva." Jeni scolded. "Esz is trying to save *her*."

The knife clattered to the floor. Kel tied off the umbilical cord. Esmeralda turned and cradled the babe close. Her color was already better. Her heart beat yet. But still she didn't cry. *Lord, please.*

Covering the babe's nose and mouth Esmeralda sucked then spit out the muck. The still form startled, drew in a breath, and released it in a wail. The entire room let out a collective breath as the girl's cries filled the room. She was surely her mother's daughter with lungs like those.

"Wash her. Water only." She handed the squalling babe to Heart. "Olva, let's move you to the bed and I'll check you."

Jeni and Esmeralda helped her, straightening the pillows making her comfortable. A few stitches and Esmeralda moved toward the door.

"Esmeralda."

She turned at Olva's call. The new mother gave a quick nod.

Esmeralda nodded back before continuing outside. She only made it a few steps into the outer room before she collapsed to her knees. Face barred in her hand and tears flowing, *Thank you, Almighty God. Thank you for new life and redemption of my past sin.*

"Is everything…" Dan's words cut off as he stood in the doorway.

Esmeralda wiped her tears and stood. "You have a beautiful daughter. The cord became wrapped around her as she came forth, and I feared… but God has been gracious. All is well."

"Thank you, m'lady. I'll wake Brother Joanis."

"'Tis the middle of the night."

"He told me to call anytime for the blessing." His last words trailed off into the dark as he rushed away.

Heart, Kel, and Jeni came beside her, wiping brows, yawning. "She asks for you." Jeni said with a squeeze of her arm.

Olva cradled her swaddled daughter. "She won't suckle."

"She has just come forth, Olva. It has been a trying ordeal for both of you."

"But she needs strength before going out into the cold night."

With a few instructions to the new mum the babe took hold of her and fed for a few moments. "See, all is well."

"All is ready." Dan burst into the room startling them both. "Joanis awaits." He stood staring at the babe.

Esmeralda took her and laid her in her father's arm. "Hold her close." She covered his arms in a thick blanket up to his shoulders. "Keep her out of the cold air and covered as much as possible."

"She's beautiful," Dan whispered peeking under the blanket again. He turned, and both Heart and Kel followed him out of the house.

"Do you wish someone to stay with you?"

Olva looked at her for a moment. "Would you stay?"

"Of course." Esz pulled up a chair and sat quietly as Olva slept, but her mind would not still. She held her cough that persisted still, even after all these weeks of teas and other remedies. MeeMa had treated many with a lingering illness. It never ended well.

Chapter 37

In the late morning, Esmeralda yawned as she strolled across a near empty town. Rain soaked through her thin gown and chemise. In the haste to reach the coming babe, she hadn't thought to bring Tio's cloak.

"M'lady?"

A man with rumpled clothes and wheat-colored hair waved her toward the gate. He was familiar. She'd served him a few times at midday. "Do you have need?" What was his name? Alfred? Albert?

"Please, m'lady, you must come. One has been injured."

"Let me collect Jeni and…" Newt was still gone as far as she knew. But if she treated the injured man outside with all the others…

"'Tis not time. I fear he may already be dead in the time it has taken me to get to you. Come."

He touched her arm. No other man here had ever touched her since she came to Rustshade. A shudder raced across her skin. "But I'll need help."

"He will die, m'lady for your delay."

Fear jolted away the apprehension and warning blaring against her reason. They rushed out the open gate to the south.

Why was the gate open with all the men gone? Where were the guards? She slowed, concern warring against her need to help.

"Take her!"

Hands clamped over her arms. A dirty cloth pushed between her lips and was tied behind her head. Though she thrashed and kicked, her arms were bound behind her and a coarse sack thrown over her head. She whimpered at the roughness. Her shoulders ached against the tightness of her bindings and her wrists burned as the abrasive rope dug into her flesh.

"Don't hurt her. The captain will have your head if she comes to him battered."

She was flung over a shoulder and bounced along until she fought the need to wretch against her gag.

They mounted horses and fled Rustshade with her draped over a man's lap. Esz lost track of how long they traveled before she was dropped to her feet only to fall back on her rump. The laughter of several men sent her heart into her throat.

Someone hauled her to her feet and she was walked a short distance only to be thrown down again. "It won't be long now, wench." It was the same voice that ordered her bound.

Tio and the war band returned to Rustshade early in the afternoon. He rolled his shoulders; a whiff of his own rank odor assaulted his nose. Covered in sweat, dust, and his enemies' blood, he could think of nothing other than jumping in the stream they use for the town's water. Well, nothing other than seeing Esmeralda. He had been gone near a fortnight and he longed to see her. Needed to be near her.

"Why are the gates flung open?" Dunlang spurred his weary horse forward to his left.

"Where are the guards?" Connin charged forward on his right.

Tio hollered orders to the men behind them. "Be alert! Look for our people. Watch for the enemy."

The men spread out with weapons drawn.

All Tio could think about was Esmeralda. *If anything has happened to her…* he cut the thought off. His heart would shatter if he lost her.

"My lords?" Connin called from the north side of the gate. "Two of our men are dead. Shot down from the wall."

"My lords, over here." The next call came from the south. Dunlang and Tio raced as the man took a knee in the rain-softened soil. His fingers outlined a slight footprint. A woman's slipper print.

"Esmeralda." The name growled between his locked jaws. "So help me if she has gone frolicking for herbs at a time like this…"

"Nay, my lord. Look." The man had followed the slender feminine impresses. "They are flanked by large boots."

He kept following the trail, losing it in the grass, then the rocks, only to pick it up again. "Father above," the soldier said.

"What?" Tio leapt from his horse as the man stepped back, crossed himself, and looked to the sky.

A disjointed array of boot prints surrounded the slight ones. Tio knew in his heart they were Esmeralda's. Her prints made long gashes in the grass. By the looks of several sunken boot impressions, she must have tried to fend off at least four large attackers. Then her prints disappeared.

Tio swung up onto the saddle and urged his horse forward as fast as was possible while still following their trail. It seemed heart-wrenchingly slow. Tio was sure he would be long dead himself before he found her.

Her captures' footsteps faded away. Her hands brushed fabric under her. Spinning around to sit on her knees, she trashed until the sack on her head fell. She sat alone in a tent shivering in her wet garments, a dirty bedroll beside her. The rain had nearly stopped as heavy steps squished through the damp soil toward the tent.

"Is she here?"

Esmeralda choked with fear at the gruff new voice. She scanned the items scattered around her.

"Aye, m'lord. She awaits your pleasure."

"Oh, she will know pleasure to be sure."

The laughter made her blood freeze within her. She squirmed frantically at her bindings, but only tore open her flesh.

"When I am finish, Alred, she will be given to the men."

Walking on her knees, she moved toward something poking out from under a pile of discarded clothes. It was a long dagger. She fumbled for the weapon with her hands behind her.

"We will see that *his* line dies here. That would-be ruler will never accept her back after we are done with her. He'll never have his needed heir. Be sure to remind them, they may treat her as they like but they may not kill her. Law dictates that he can't put her aside and continue to lead, but we will have to capture the next wench he selects if this one dies."

Frantically Esmeralda sliced at the ropes, and cut as much of her own flesh as she did the bindings. It took far too long to sever them.

The voices went silent outside and footsteps approached the tent.

As last, the binding loosened enough for her to wrench one hand out of the ropes. In one movement, she shook her other hand free, rose to her feet, untied the gag, and moved to the back of the tent. She thrust the knife in the fabric and pulled down. *Please let them not hear this.*

A cavernous gorge lay five wagon lengths before her. Rocky ground lay to her right.

"She escapes!" The bellow came from the leader behind her.

The signal, like a ruckus owl hooting, drew Tio's gaze to Connin who waved for the war band to come toward him.

Shafts of white peeked through the thick trees. Tio's men inched forward again. They spread out and circled wide to take the enemy from all sides as the leader of the Force of Echoes returned. He stopped outside a tent and talked to someone Tio could not see. As they came to the last of the trees and prepared to leap into battle, the leader turned and drew back his tent flap. He roared so it drowned out the earlier laughter.

"She escapes!"

Tio's men burst into the tent-filled clearing as his enemy leapt up and gave chase away from them.

Esz didn't look back to see how many pursued her. Yanking up her hem, she dug in her toes and charged at the wide gap. Did she hear water? Or was that only her own blood thundering in her ear? It didn't matter. She knew what lay behind her. She either leapt out as far as she could praying there was a river deep enough not to kill her when she landed, or she would be ravaged by the many men charging behind her.

Her legs burned, but the ground shook with their pounding steps.

Two wagon lengths before the edge. Their roars were right behind her. The rasping of her own breath triggered the coughing again.

One wagon length. She could see part way down on the other side. Mayhaps it was not as deep as she feared.

Three more strides.

Two.

Esmeralda burst from behind a tent running like the devil himself chased her—which by the look on the faces of the Force of Echoes, he did. But she ran directly at Miseries Gorge. How many of his people had shattered their body on the jagged rocks far below?

He spurred his horse forward, barely able to cry her name as she charged for the edge.

"Esmeralda!" Tio's pained roar pulled her up. She twisted. He charged toward her, sword cutting down every enemy in his path. But he was too far away.

She twisted. But too late.

Her arms flayed out beside her, fighting to find her balance.

She'd gone too fast.

Turned too suddenly.

She tipped over the edge. Eyes full of fear screaming his name.

A blood rage like he had never experience exploded in his veins. He cut down anything that crossed his path. *Kill them. Kill them all.*

Chapter 38

Cold air tore at her cloths and hair, until Esmeralda's arm slammed into something spinning her to the side. Sharp leaves raked her face. A branch cut her cheek. Another opened a gash in her arm. She grasped for anything solid to cling to.

Her right hand clutched a thin branch. She landed hard on her side driving out all air. Eyes squeezed closed against the pain bolting around her battered body. She forced herself to hold firm to the branch in her hand, despite the piece of wood jutting out and pushing a hole into her palm. Blood dripped down her arm.

She lay still and dragged a tentative breath into her tight lungs. Coughed. And the coughing continued. Her body shook making the leaves dance around her. The clash of swords and roar of men filtered down to her. With some effort she cracked one eye open.

She lay in a tree growing sideways from the cliff-face. It jutted out trying in vain to right itself. With both eyes now open, she found herself on a large limb with her foot almost touching the wide trunk. The edge she'd fallen from lay only twice her height above.

She dared to glance down. Only rock filled her vision—jagged and deadly. The leaves shuddered again as her eyes clamped closed. She clung to the branch unable to move to even wiggle her toe.

The battle still raged above. Tio roared above the din. Would she be safer here? She glanced again over her shoulder at the certain death that lay below. She pressed her face against the back of her hands as they clung to the branch. No water lay below, only huge spiked rocks like a dragon's open jaws ready to devour her.

There were no other trees anywhere in the ragged gorge. Only this lone protector struggling against its own fall. "Thank You, Lord," she whispered.

She remained there unmoving as a breeze sent free strands of her hair across her face. "Lord," she choked unable to say more for the tears and terror gripping her.

The tree jolted and rocks dislodged raining down on her. She couldn't stay here. The lone tree was loosing its precarious grip on the cliff side. It shuddered again as she shifted with all due care.

Esmeralda crawled along the trunk, held her breath against any further coughs, grabbed an exposed root, and pulled herself to her feet. Enough roots and rocks lay between her and the edge that she thought she might be able to climb. When she reached her left arm up to grasp a rock above her, bolts of pain had her returning it to cradle against her body. As hard as she had landed it was very likely broken.

The tree jerked again, exposing more roots.

Up. She had to go up.

The tree slipped further toward the canyon's mouth. Mud oozed from around the roots toward the trunk.

Now. She had to move now.

She pressed her back against the roots and looped her stronger arm through a twisting vine-like root. Her cough would not quiet and the tree shook with each one. She pulled the skirt of her gown back between her legs and tied the hem around her waist at her belly. Her legs lay exposed below the knees. Tio would have a fit about not being *proper* but as the tree slipped more she had no other options.

More mud escaped and cascaded over her.

She took a step and her smooth sole glanced off the bark toppling her balance. She crouched to keep from falling, but didn't dare linger to steady her breath as another tremor rumbled beneath her.

She kicked off her shoes, not watching where they fell, and yanked off her hose, tearing gashes in her legs with her nails. Before the next shudder hit, she worked herself up into the roots and onto the rocks. Her injured arm could hold her in place but not hoist her up. The blood on her other palm ran from the gash in her forearm and slickened her grip.

She needed to work quickly, but with her injured arm, the blood, the coughing, and the bark cutting into her feet she slipped repeatedly. She'd gone barefoot most of her life. How had her feet softened so much in her leather slippers in mere months?

She caught herself as she tumbled again. She spun dangerously on the ball of one foot, only her strong arm kept her from falling. She twisted until she slammed her wounded arm into the rocky cliff face and cried out. Tears blurred her vision. She knew she had to get clear of the tree before it pulled the whole cliff side down with her.

She thought the edge was only an arm-length away. Steadying herself against the thinning roots and blinking at the rocks and mud falling on her, she looped her sore arm as an anchor and threw up her good hand.

The tree nearly broke free beneath her.

She cried out as she began to fall.

A massive hand encircled her out-stretched wrist and yanked her up.

Chapter 39

In a single heartbeat, Esmeralda flew over the cliff edge and slammed into Tio's chest. One arm encircled her waist. The other forced her head under his chin. His lips pressed to her hair and remained there. His rapid hot breath caressed her scalp. He trembled more than she did.

"Eszy." Tears choked his words. He swallowed hard, but his voice grew no steadier. "Are you hurt?"

Smashed against him as she was, she couldn't speak, or cough, and she couldn't move. She could barely draw a shallow breath. Her hands were pinned between them and she tried to wiggle one free. Tap on his chest. Something to ease he grip.

He groaned as he relaxed his hold. She held up her bloody and torn wrists and hands. He drew back further to take them, but gasped when he saw her exposed legs. "Esmeralda! Cover up."

She stepped beside him to keep from tumbling back into the gorge and untied her hem. "I couldn't very well climb with it slipping me up."

"You should have waited—"

A low rumble interrupted him, and they pulled back from the edge as the tree that had saved her tore a goodly portion of the cliff away.

"No, I could not have," she whispered with a shudder, coughing again.

Tio took one of her hands gently and raised her chin with his other. His gaze sparkled with fear. "Did they … Did they *hurt* you, Esmeralda?"

"No. Though was their sole intent for taking me. Their lord told his men they would all have a go at me after."

White hot angry flashed in his eyes and she tried to pull from him. His grip hardened and exploded with heat.

She slammed against his chest, stealing her breath. "You're hurting me," she whimpered.

He didn't budge.

She reached out a trembling hand and stroked his cheek. It was caked in grim and gore. "Tiobald?"

He blinked at last.

"Tio?"

His gaze shifted and focused on her again.

"You're hurting me," she whispered again.

His grip slackened, but he didn't release her. "They did not take you?"

"No." She tried to pull from him again. "They didn't want me dead. They were to ruin me, so that 'his line would die here.' I assume he referred to you. Your line."

The rage returned to his eyes. "Aye." His words were hoarse and strained. "They know well as long as you live, I will take no other as wife. And they know our laws that I could nay claim you as wife again if they had…"

His gaze again took in the whole of her. "But they didn't—"

She jerked her hand free biting her lip against the pain. "I am hail. I am as untouched as last you saw me. Though now that I have been captive of these vile men, I know you will never believe me." Her anger collided with her pain making her voice ragged, far too high, and she started her coughing again.

Horses thundered through the trees, and she whirled with a yelp. But it was the men of Rustshade.

"M'lady!" they shouted as the caught sight of her. But their gazes narrowed and darted between her and Tio.

She stomped her foot. "I am whole. Untouched. Not defiled!"

Each of the men relaxed as their collective sigh filled the clearing.

"Come, Esmeralda." Neither his tone nor his grip on her arm was kind.

Two more horses charged up. "M'lord, Dunlang chases after the few who escaped. He bids you come seek your revenge."

The other rider lowered a limp body to the ground. "M'lady, he's injured." They looked her over quickly. "Forgive us, m'lady. Might you be hale enough to tend to Rogga? We have tried, but are unable to stop the blood?"

She pulled to tend the man who had helped save her, but Tio yanked her back. "He can be treated in Rustshade where our lady will be safe."

"Nay, m'lord. 'Tis a grievous wound. He dies now."

She twisted free with a yelp and stumbled a few steps before she knelt next to Rogga. His thigh gushed blood.

"Esmeralda." He growled.

"Tio." She answered him with a growl of her own as she wiped her hands of her own blood on Tio's trousers. *Why would the cough not be still?*

Several of the men cleared their throats and either covered their mouths or turned away. But she saw the mirth in their eyes.

Chapter 40

Though battered and bruised herself, and her tattered fingers fumbled, Esmeralda managed to stop Rogga's bleeding. "This should be enough until we get him safe inside the palisade for me to finish with Jeni's help." She rubbed her aching arm, glad it seemed free from a break.

As she stood, an arm clamped around her waist and she found herself lifted onto Tio's lap. They rode his roan back toward the town.

"You should join Dunlang."

"Why? Why did you go? Why do you continue to be so reckless and put yourself in danger?"

"One of the men said someone was injured. Begged me to go to him before he died."

"One of my men? Who?"

Esmeralda tried to get comfortable. "Can I not ride behind you?"

His arm tightened around her. "Who lured you to your doom?"

"Short, sits in the back of the common room on the north side, but only occasionally. I think his name is Alfred. Never seen him anywhere else in the shire." She shifted again. "Tio, the shire is there. Your injured come behind us. I'll walk the rest of the way and you go to Dunlang. Let him not fall to those venomous snakes."

He held her tighter. "I will care for you." His gaze remained straight ahead; his words still harsh.

"Why? I am soiled beyond redemption in your eyes. What does it matter what happens to me now?"

"You are mine." His arm tightened again as the possessiveness of his tone vibrated against her skin.

"But you don't want me." Her cough grew persistent.

His next words caressed her neck, husky and so intense they made her shudder. "I have always wanted *you*, Eszy."

She looked up at him. Searching his face. "Tio?"

Something rumbled through his chest, whether groan or moan or growl, was unclear.

Moments later he carried her in the house, dropped her to her feet, and thrust her an arm's length away. "You are forbidden to leave this home."

"But my patients—"

"I. DO. NOT. CARE!" His roar blew whips of her hair from her face. His arms were rigid and clenched tight at his sides. "You are drenched. Your cough worsens. You were captured and held. You are torn to shreds."

"And defiled, don't forget."

"No. You said no."

She put her fists on her hips. "Would be easy enough to prove I am still a maiden."

"I believe they did not harm you like they intended."

"Then let me go out and—"

"You will stay here if I have to nail that door closed."

"Then you might as well draw your sword and cut me down now for I shall die locked in here."

"Esz? M'lady?" A voice called from outside the door.

"Jeni, come." Tio said as he jerked open the door. "Treat Esz's injures, stay with her as long as Zeke will allow. And do NOT allow her out of this home until I return."

Esmeralda screaked her frustration but he slammed the door.

Tio put his heels to a fresh mount and charged back toward the fleeing enemy. He collected his men as he went. They had staggered themselves along the route so he easily joined up with Dunlang before the sunset.

"Tio. Glad I am to have you again beside me." He put his hand on Tio's shoulder. "Sore I am for the loss of your Esmeralda. We shall honor her right—"

"She lives."

Dunlang staggered back a step. "Praise the Almighty." He considered Tio. "Is she… whole?"

"She swears aye."

"You don't believe her?"

"I do. We arrived at the same moment as their leader. He had not the time before she escaped. Though it may no longer matter if these escape and spread the lie amongst the people that they did in fact all have a go at her as they intended."

Dunlang crossed his arms. "Explain."

"She overheard the leader say they were not to kill her so that 'his line will end here.'"

"They cannot fight us directly in honorable battle, so they stoop to stealing your wife and dishonoring her?"

Tio could only nod. His blood rage scorched his skin and narrowed his vision.

A cool hand lay on his shoulder again. "Well, if as I suspect, you have not lain with her, it would be easy enough for a physician to prove."

"She said as much, but I believe her. Our men do as well. She did not behave as one inured in such a horrific manor."

"Then our course is set, death of those who intended to do this wicked thing."

Tio nodded. "The traitor Alred is mine. He will curse the day he was born. And he will tell me what made him betray us."

Dunlang waved the men over. "Time to drive these rats from their holes." He took a knee and with his finger in the mud he laid out their attack.

Tio barely listened. He didn't need more than to be pointed in the right direction. He'd remove the head of every man who was involved in capturing his Eszy.

Chapter 41

"'Tis good to see you, Tio." She looked thinner and paler. She was not well.

"Come, sit, eat more than the drop you normally favor."

"Then what?"

The fear in her eyes crushed his heart. "All I want is you always beside me." He stood offering her the gift he had brought.

She stared at it. "What is it?"

He smiled, "A gift, of course."

"Why?"

"'Tis the Christ Mass."

She stepped back from the gift, fingers covering her mouth, shaking her head. "I can't."

"Why ever not?"

She looked at him, tears pooling. "I have nothing for you."

Tio reached for her, allowing one finger to brush her cheek—like satin under his rough calluses. She leaned into him. He let his hand cradle her face, and her eyes closed. "You are my gift, Eszy." The words echoed in the room and in his soul.

Her gaze searched his. She stood utterly still. He brushed her cheek again and smiled as he leaned forward, his lips brushing hers…

Tio jerked from his sleep. Torn free of the dream again, his heart thundered and he shivered against the chill his sweat-covered tunic caused. He held his aching head in his hands. Every part of him missed her—needed her—wanted her. And here he chased after those who wished to destroy them. He, Dunlang, and their men had taken all but three of the Force of Echoes. He was now more than a week's ride from her. The dreams of holding her and kissing her, had been infrequent at first. Now they came every time he dared close his eyes.

Word came through their men in both Haven and Rustshade; Garrett had returned to his work on the wall. Olva's babe, Mary, now the second born alive, added to their number. Jeni and Heart were both with child. It was time to conquer his fear and return to the woman he loved —if she would still have him.

Tio had not returned that night. Jeni had tended her many injures. Though her capture, escape, and fall had battered her body, mercifully none of her bones were broken. While Jeni nursed her over the next few days, Esz used the larger bed not wanting her friend to know the troubles between her and Tio. Esz tried to see Rogga, but Newt saw to his care and reported to her that he healed well.

As Tio failed to return and Esz's cough worsened, she allowed Jeni to tend her less and less. In the last days, she'd forbid Jeni from entering Tio's home for fear of the fever and Jeni being with child. He hadn't shown his face in near a fortnight. Esmeralda kept herself in bed.

The cough that had begun as an annoying tickle was now deep, wet, and unending. This morning as she pushed off her bed in the middle room, the cough continued. She lowered the cloth she held to her mouth. Little crimson droplets dotted it. She sagged against the doorframe of her isolated chamber. Her loneliness didn't matter any longer. Her end would soon come.

Wrapping herself in Tio's cloak, she stepped outside. The bleak sky mirrored her mood. The drizzle collected like a heavy mist, chilling her further. "Newt?"

"Aye, m'lady."

"I need your help."

The young man, who spent far more time with her than her husband did, stepped from under the eaves and pushed back his cowl. His light hair and well-trimmed beard and moustache framed an attractive face. He would make some woman very happy. "Anything, m'lady."

After another coughing spasm, she looked at him. "I need your oath, Newt, that what I ask of you, you will never share with Tio or any other in the shire."

He shifted his weight between his feet and stared at the ground. "M'lady, I…"

"'Tis for his own good. Truly. What I do now will save his life—all your lives."

Newt stared long at her before inclining his head. "You have my oath, m'lady."

She suffered through more coughing, ribs and back aching, and leaned against the door for support before she spoke again. "I must leave Rustshade. And it must be now."

Chapter 42

The remaining members of the Echoes lie dead at his feet. Tio wiped his sword and turned toward home eager to be under a solid roof and not in a tent. But more than walls and the comfort of his home, he wanted to claim his wife as he should have from the beginning. Rain fled from the sky in rivers. Winters in this apart of the realm were mild. Few times could he remember such a storm.

"Are you sure you wish to leave now?" Connin led his horse to him. "The storm will pass, then we can travel more quickly."

"I have been too long from home."

Connin handed up the reins, squinting against the torrent. "I feared you would reject her forever."

"I did not reject her. I chose her. I've provided for her, protected her. Well, I have tried to protect her."

"But have you loved her?"

"With all my heart."

"Does she know that?"

"She will soon." Tio pressed his horse into motion with his heels. The charger hung its head against the deluge of water and slogged forward. His hooves added a squishing and sucking sound to the endless cadence of falling water. Tio didn't dare spur him to speed for fear the soft soil would cause the animal to stumble and them both be injured.

"God bless our journey, my friend. We will follow soon," Connin called out.

The slow plod through the valleys and glens gave Tio ample time to think. Too much time. How many others had taken note of his mistreatment of Esmeralda? How many now held him in disdain because of it? He had been a fool. *Lord, let there be time to set things to right.*

The rain never relented. He was soaked through to the bone when he led the horse through the door in the gate late in the evening near a week later. His heart summersaulted at the mere thought of seeing Esmeralda. It thrilled to think of holding her, kissing her. He slipped several times in the mud as he hurried to stable the horse next to his roan before racing to her.

His home lay dark as he approached. Not even a candle flickered. "Newt?" There was no answer. He pushed open the door. No warmth lay within. No live coals remained in the hearth. "Esz?" He lit a candle leaving a trail of water as he searched the rooms calling her name.

Three hard hits with his shoulder and he opened the third sealed room. Now shrouded in dust, the cradle and items his sister had collected for the birth of her first child remained where he'd thrown them years ago.

"Esmeralda?"

A package sat bound on the table. He pulled the string and revealed a finely stitched tunic. She had given him a Christ Mass gift. But where was she now?

He raced to Newt's and pounded on the door. He entered when no one answered, but his faithful squire was not at home either. A few warm embers remained in the ashes. He had not been gone as long as Eszy it would seem. There'd been a fire here this morning.

The rain fell in gentle droplets as he stood outside searching the darkness. Where could she be? His heart fell like a weight to the pit of his stomach. Could they have run off together? Forsaken her vows for another after he had thought her fallen? Another who would love her as she deserved and not hold her to the law of her station?

He raced to yet another home. *Bam, bam, bam.* "Zeke? Jeni?" The door creaked. A candle flame wavered against the cold air flooding the room through the opening.

"M'lord?" Zeke looked out and pulled the door open a little more.

"Esmeralda. Do you know where she is?"

"What do mean where she is?" Jeni called from the darkness. "She's not at home?"

"Nay. The house is cold and empty. Neither can I find Newt."

Jeni's face peeked round her husband. Her disheveled braid dangled over her shoulder. "Do not go making further accusations on her honor, m'lord. Neither of them would ever betray you."

"Then where are they? Did she not say anything to you?"

"Nay, m'lord. I haven't seen Esz… m'lady, in several days. The cough worsened and a fever beset her. She forbade me tend her since I am with child."

"Days?"

"Aye," Zeke said wrapping an arm around his shivering wife. "She did not come to chapel on the Lord's Day last."

Tio turned back to the darkness and staggered away. A slender shaft of moonlight caught on the soaked figure lumbering through the door in the gate. Tio ran to him. "Newt!" The young man was as drenched as he was. "Where is Esmeralda?"

Newt would not look up. "I gave my oath to her not so say."

Tio seized him by the shoulders and shook. "Tell me where my wife is."

"I cannot, m'lord."

"She is my wife, man."

Newt looked up, holding him in a hard stare. "Is she? You show her no affection. Leave her here to waste away, abandoned, alone under the taint of having been assaulted."

Terror gripped Tio till he wanted to wretch. "Tell me she is still my wife."

"She would take no other. She's a godly woman. Ferociously fought off those who would defile her. But you know her not at all if you must ask."

The next thought turned him to ice. Jeni had said her illness had worsened. "Does she still live?" The words were a choked whisper.

Newt again stared at the ground rocking between his feet. He offered a single nod. "Just."

Again, Tio grabbed him. "Tell me where she is that I may go to her and aid her."

Tears, not rain, now wet Newt's face when he looked up. "She is dying. She refuses anyone to tend her for fear they will fall ill as well. She will not allow it. And I have given my oath to aid her in this last request."

Tio doubled in pain, his hands braced on his knees. All he'd so foolishly done to keep her from dying and still she was leaving him. And she did so all alone.

"You must tell me where she is. She can't be left on her own."

"Nay. I will not go back on my word."

Tio stared, angered by Newt's refusal and grateful for the man's brotherly love of Esmeralda. His heart shattered and he couldn't draw an even breath. Tears burned. Where had she gone? She feared any other getting sick. Newt had come through the gate—without a horse. "The old hunter's cottage."

Newt's head dropped. "I did not tell you."

"No, but you will return with me." Tio grabbed him by the elbow and pulled him toward the stables.

Newt tried to pull free. "She forbade it."

Tio stopped and gripped him by both arms. "I will die with her rather than let her suffer alone. Pray there is something yet to be done."

"M'lord, you cannot. What of your people?"

"I will give it all away for her."

"You know what will become of us if you do not take your rightful place."

He paused for a moment. The entire kingdom or the woman he loved. None of them would survive if she did not recover. She was the heart to his brute force. "We save her, then we claim our place once again."

They saddled their horses, ran to the gate, led the horses through the smaller opening before mounting, and charged around the wall to the north. Stars danced between the clouds with a waning moon as the leaning mud structure came into view. Tio spurred his mount ahead, and leapt from the charging horse before it fully stopped.

He burst through the door. Esmeralda shielded her face. She was a ghost of the woman he had chosen. Skin ashen, hair disheveled, but the worst was her deep, rattling breaths.

She gasped, coughed, and croaked out one word. "Stop."

Chapter 43

The pounding of hooves outside had awakened her. She knew before he smashed open the door that Tio had found her.

"Stop. Come no closer."

"Esmeralda I will not—"

"Get out."

"Nay. You are my wife. And I love you."

She was so stunned even her coughing abated for several moments. "You never wanted me," she whispered at last.

He closed the door and knelt in front of her. She pulled away, terrified he would become sick as well. "I told you true when I said I never wanted to *choose anyone* at all. But Eszy, when I walked that line of possible wives and you stared so boldly, challenging me to take you over the others, from that moment I wanted *you*."

The lingering sickness ravaging her body left her weak and her mind muddled. She tried to shake it clear only to stir another fit of coughs. "You despise my very touch."

He reached for her, but she jerked away. "I feared the power of your touch."

She looked at him without comprehension.

"I have desired you since we kissed. Wanted desperately to share the marriage bed with you. And I knew if you but touched me, I would not be able to stop myself, and then I would break my vow to always keep you safe."

"I don't understand."

"As Second, and sheriff, as you say, I have gone on every choosing. I have watched each of our men go out and select a woman full of health and life. As Second, I have watched over the couple, protected them and watched as they each woman became a treasured member of our community. Only to listen to her writhe in agonizing pain when she could not bring forth the child within her. I heard it first in my mother. Then my sister. It is the most heartbreaking sound and the most helpless I have ever been. I could not do that to you."

"But Ido and Mary?"

"Aye, because of you, things have changed. But still I feared."

"Would have been better to have died loved, than like this."

"Forgive me, please, Eszy."

She nodded through another spasm of coughs. "You have said your peace. I forgive you. Now you must leave."

He did not retreat but came closer. He sat beside her bedroll, his back against the wall and pulled her into his lap. "I'll never leave you again."

She struggled to break his hold but it only made her cough more. She snatched up a cloth, and pressed it to her mouth.

"Shhh. Eszy." He kissed the top of her head. "You'll not get rid of me this time. I'll never be such a fool again."

Through the cloth she whispered, "Then you will die too."

"If God wills it. But I'll not let go of you."

She relaxed and leaned her head against his chest. One arm wrapped securely around her as the other stroked her arm. Tears sprang forth, searing her already raw throat. "This is all I ever wanted."

He kissed her head again. "Forgive me, my love."

"I don't want you to die."

"Then fight. Use that incredible knowledge of yours and find a way to heal yourself. Let me truly show you how much I love you."

She pulled the cloth from her mouth showing him the bloodstains. "'Tis too late. A sickness of the lungs like this cannot be cured."

He pulled her chin up. "There is a way. I'm sure of it. You know something to try, something that would seem utterly contradictory. Like cutting a babe from a womb. But something that will work. Fight for me, Eszy. Come home with me that I may love you all my days. Help me be the man I need to be for our people."

She shook her heard.

"Something you learned from a merchant in the tavern?"

She stilled.

"That. Whatever you are thinking… do that." He kissed her head again. "Please, try."

"'Tis pointless—"

"If you live to bring forth my children, will nay be pointless."

"Children?"

"Aye, several. Strong and smart, like their mum."

"Mum." The word danced inside her. But could there be any chance for her? Did she know enough to try? Did she possess the strength to fight? He still held her. His strong heart pounding against her frail frame seemed enough to give them both life. What did she have to lose in trying? Only hope.

"It will require some work, and I can't promise I have the strength to survive long enough to even begin."

"Tell me what must be done. And we'll pray God gives you strength and fully restores you."

Chapter 44

Tio thought he knew fear. But nothing compared to listening to Esz fight for each breath or to see her strength leech out of her at each coughing spasm. She was weaker than most of the women they had lost in childbirth. She coughed so hard her lungs bled.

Please, Lord, let her live.

He laid her down. The pain of leaving her, even for moments, tore his beating heart from his chest as he stepped outside. Newt seemed to be asleep in his saddle.

"Wake up, my friend."

"Is she…?"

"Nay, she still draws breath, though it be a ragged one. I need your help. She has an idea, but we must hurry." The man nodded now fully alert. "Gather as many of our men as you can roust at this early hour. We need to patch these walls and seal all the holes. We need all the skins Lew has to cover the thatch without bringing it down on our heads. When the patches are complete, I'll need wood, short, long-burning pieces with sap that will burn hot." I need three large water barrels filled here by the door, a bucket, and a ladle. No one is to enter but me. Bring her healing bag and ask Jeni to make a marrow broth for her.

Tio handed the reins of his horse to Newt with a final list of needed items and the young man disappeared into the darkness. Tio paused only a moment to listened to Eszy's labored breathing before scouring the surrounding area for stones. He laid them aside in the cottage and dug a circular trench in the earthen floor near her mat. He heaped the dirt he removed in the middle before taking the larger rocks and straddling the groove he'd cut. He stacked the smaller stones on them, leaving the middle open. Adding some of the kindling from the pile near the hearth to the center of the ring, he struck the flint as he heard the work outside begin to fortify and seal the structure. As the flames grew, the rocks began to glow with the heat they collected.

"Water, m'lord." Newt whispered.

Before opening the door, Tio warned. "Make sure none comes near."

"Aye."

The sun's first rays were kissing the sky as Tio carried in a bucket full of water and Eszy's herbs. Setting them where he could reach easily, he pulled out the items she had told him and added them to the water. Next, he sat beside he and pulled her into his lap again. Her shoulder tucked against his ribs and her head under his chin.

She stirred. "You need not hold me."

"I have wasted enough time. You'll remain in my arms till you are strong enough to pull from them. Besides, even I know a cough is helped by sitting up."

"And if I don't wish to be out of your arms?"

He kissed her head. "Then I shall never let you go." He dipped a ladle in the bucket and slowly poured the water over the stones. It hissed and sizzled filling the cramped room with steam and the scent of eucalyptus and cloves. A few more ladles, and the room was heavy with the warm moisture he prayed would help her lungs rid themselves of the sickness.

"Since you are awake, Jeni has prepared the broth for you."

She took a few ragged sips.

"I'd also like you to eat a little of this." He held up the robust cheese she hated.

She buried her face in his chest and shook her head.

He stroked her back with a light chuckle. "I know 'tis not your favorite, but we swear it is what keeps us so hale. Have you treated any colds or fever in any man in Rustshade?"

Again, she shook her head, but her face stayed hidden.

"Just a few bits." Still she didn't move. "I have cenderberry mead to wash it down." A smile pulled at his tunic and her head at last lifted. "I know 'tis your favorite."

With trembling fingers, she broke off a tiny piece of the cheese, tipped back her head, and swallowed it whole. Still she shuddered and grimaced.

"'Tis not so bad."

"And you thought the well water tasted fine."

He chuckled and made her take another bite before offering her the mead. He managed to get her to take a little more of the broth before she slept again.

He ladled more water on the rocks, leaned back his head, and began his vigil.

When the hissing of the steam died away, he heard Brother Joanis praying fervently. Tio only caught fragments of it as the holy man walked continuously around the cottage. "Lord, You say that You heal and none can be taken from Your hand… Have mercy on our dear sister… Those who hold her dear have great need of this lady… Mercy and healing will come in the name of Christ…"

"Stay with me, Eszy. I can't bear to live without you." *Please, Lord. Save her. Let me redeem the ills I have caused her. Let me be released from the fool I have been.*

Chapter 45

Esmeralda fought for every breath. Her entire body ached. But Tio was here. He held her against his beating heart. He cared for her and fought to get her well. She didn't believe it possible she would recover from bleeding lungs. No one ever had. But then, she never believed Tio loved her, and yet here he was risking his own life to be with her. Fear, not disgust had kept him away. He didn't want to lose her. They may not win this fight, but she clung to the possibility she might yet be a true wife and even a mother.

Tio laid her down. His hand came under her skirts and pushed them up.

"You want the marriage bed now?" It hurt to talk, and her voice was little more than a harsh whisper.

"Oh, Eszy, I have always wanted to lie with you. This, though, is merely removing your clothes." He pushed her dress and her chemise over her head and pulled them off her arms.

"Why?"

He again cradled her against his heart. His bare chest damp and sticky. "The room is hot but you shiver. The moisture clings to your clothes and chills you. You said something about the heat driving out the sickness. I think it must be done without the layers of fabric."

At last, she lay skin to skin in nothing but her undergarments with her husband. He again ladled the water, and the steam clung to her. A gulp of cool fresh air seemed like a dream of a man dying of thirst.

Surely this was not the cure for the sickness of the lungs. She curled into Tio, trying to commit every sensation of him to her addled thoughts before she lost her fight.

Esmeralda slipped further away, stirring only rarely as he retrieved buckets and fed the fire. But she didn't wake fully again, nor did she speak or even open her eyes. Each time she roused even a little, Tio made her take some broth and more of the hateful cheese. He resorted to crumbling it in the broth. Even in her barely conscious state, she crinkled her nose and shuddered at the taste.

Time blurred.

The room was heavy and oppressive. It didn't seem likely that so much moisture could drive out the wetness inside her. But he did as she had instructed and he prayed. Having her cradled against was like pressing a branding iron to his chest. She radiated heat like the rocks did. Soon he was drinking as much water as he ladled on the stones.

Tio woke to the fire within the stones nearly out. He hadn't slept that long in days. Eszy hadn't coughed as much. He placed his hand on her back. It rattled less as she breathed. *Oh please, Lord.* Hope soared in him like a hawk loosed to the heavens as he rebuilt the fire.

When next he woke, Eszy breathed with ease and the fever had, at last, broken. The worst over, he laid her down and let the fire within the stones die as he kindled a more reasonable heat from the hearth at the end of the room. She rested peacefully as he stepped outside and spoke with Newt. The shire would want to know, so preparations for her homecoming could begin.

As Newt rode off, Tio stretched his cramped muscles before kneeling in the grass. He lifted his hands to the heavens. "Thank you. Thank you, my God. I was a fool to waste the blessing you showered on my life. Help me be the man she needs and let me never forget what I could have lost. Help me to treasure her as a precious jewel from Your hand. Thank you, Lord." He remained until the cool air drove him back to the fire and her side where he waited for her to wake.

Chapter 46

Esmeralda drifted on a gentle wave. Soon she'd reach the shore, open her eyes, and be in paradise. Her pain and illness had slipped away in the void between heaven and earth. She was left now in the stillness with the sweet memory of Tio's embrace. His professions of love and his tender kisses had allowed her to release her former life in peace. Soon. Soon she would wake to a new life.

Strange how she yet heard his heartbeat, a complimentary pulse to her own. Did one have a heartbeat in heaven? At last her muscles responded to her, and she rolled them in a gentle lazy stretch.

A strong band tightened around her waist, and pain stabbed through her left side. Mayhaps she wasn't in paradise. A shudder danced down her spine and the band tightened again. If she had indeed been damned for her role in Olva's mum's death, she would expect pain as well as wailing and gnashing of teeth. The air she drew into her lungs, though with some pain, remained sweet and tinted with eucalyptus and cloves. Hardly the scent she'd expect in hell.

The void beckoned again. Mayhaps she still lingered between the former life and the next. She'd rest now. All would be made clear soon.

Esmeralda drew in a deep full breath and winced. Clear air filled her lungs and her muscles rippled as she pulled from the abyss. The ache in her side renewed its displeasure at waking. And again, the band tightened around her. As her mind came to life again, she also realized she needed to relieve herself.

The Holy Scriptures spoke of the next life as being devoid of pain and sorrow. Yet her ribs burned and her heart cried for another day with Tio—the man who did indeed love her. And she couldn't bring herself to envision chamber pots in heaven. But she surely needed one now.

She commanded her muscles to action again. The band holding her firm rippled and a warm kiss pressed to the skin between her shoulders and her neck. She forced an eye open. Light flickered from a fire over rough mud walls. She wasn't in paradise or hell. She was alive. With a very full bladder.

She squirmed again trying to coordinate muscles that were stiff from disuse.

A puff of warm air caressed her shoulder before another kiss. The form behind her came to life with a lazy stretch. The next kiss was followed by a tender voice humming against her skin. "Are you at last awake, my love?"

Not just alive, but in Tio's arms. She caressed the hand clamped firmly around her. If she dreamed, she never wanted to wake. But this wasn't a dream of her lonely heart. He truly had come for her and loved her.

She rolled to her back to looked up at him as air whistled through her teeth. He rose on his elbow. He wore a loose tunic not tucked into his breeches. She was in a clean chemise. A stabbing pain exploded in her side.

His hand, that had been resting on her belly, traced where her fingers explored her ribs. He brows scrunched together. "You're still in pain."

"I think my ribs are broken."

"How?" His touch was intoxicating. Like too much mead, she floated on a sea of pleasure and giddy emotions. Her skin warmed and tingled.

His hand moved from her ribs to cradle her cheek, his gaze intent.

"Eszy, how did you break your ribs?"

Did it matter? He was here beside her.

He smiled, his thumb caressing her cheek. "If you keep looking at me like that, I shall not be able to resist you any longer." His hand moved from her check to her side. She flinched. And the scowl returned. "Do you hurt in other places?"

She shook her head and tried to push herself up. Her arms trembled and her ribs stabbed, and she lowered herself again for a moment. "I am in need of the chamber pot," she whispered, heat flooding her cheeks.

His smile returned and he gently sat her up on the raised bed where they'd been sleeping. As she looked at it trying to remember if it had been in the hut when she'd arrived, he scooped her up into his arms and carried her to the corner. There, over the pot, sat the chair with much of the seat removed that she had brought to Kel's home. He supported her while she arranged her garments, then left the hut. He returned moments later with an armful of wood.

Adding some to the fire, he stacked the rest beside it. He came to her where she still sat, too weak to even stand. He raised her arms to around his neck, then pulled her up. Her head dropped to his chest, his strong heart pounding against her ear. Her entire body quaked with a weakness she couldn't image.

A kiss pressed to the top of her head as he provided support. "Now, can you tell me how you broke your ribs?"

"It has been known to happen with violent coughing, though the fall over the cliff may have been the start of the problem. I did not think them broken but…"

He caressed her back and she melted into him; her fingers lost their grip and her hands slid down to his chest. Hard muscles lay well formed under his tunic. She traced each one.

Tio moved her toward a table. She stiffened, fear clawing at her again.

He made her pull her chemise up so as not to sit on it. "Do you have anything in your bag to wrap around you until they heal?" He'd taken a step away.

She shivered in his absence. Thoughts fled and her eyes closed.

His fingers caressed her hands and she looked at them. One gripped hers as a finger raised her chin until his gaze captured hers. She wanted to reach out to him. Touch his face. But if he pulled from her again, she would shatter.

He raised the hand he held and kissed her palm before pressing it to his check. "Your touch lights a fire in me. A fire that will consume us both. For now you have much healing to do." His hand left hers still on his cheek and brushed over her ribs.

Pain shot through her and she jerked.

He pressed his forehead to hers. "If even a light touch brings you such pain, lying with me would be unbearable. Now, do you have something to bind them?" he asked again.

"There should be lengths of cloth in my satchel."

He rose, pulling from her. The emptiness did not return however. When he came back with the binding, she lifted her garment. Her hipbones, knees, and ribs jutted out from pale skin. She gasped.

He cradled her cheek. "Food and time will restore you." He bound her securely before standing. "Sit there a moment and I'll warm some food." As he moved about dropping items from a basket into pots and pans, he asked. "What is the proper treatment to restore strength in someone who has lingered ill for a long time?"

"How long?"

He glanced over his shoulder. "You have been here over a fortnight."

She gasped but regretted it. "Near a month in total. I shouldn't be alive at all."

"I praise God that He returned you to me." He left the food

unattended, knelt before her and gripped her hands. "I will spend the rest of my days making things right between us."

She pulled one hand free and touched his cheek. His whiskers were long, becoming unruly like when they had met. He kissed her palm again. "Forgive me for doubting," she whispered.

"Forgive my fear and neglect."

With slow movement, breathing through the pain, she brought her lips to his. He rose on his knees and met her. The tender press of skin deepened, his mouth covered hers, his fingers slid into her hair, pressing her closer. His kiss became hungry, wild, as his other arm wrapped around her and pulled her.

She gasped in pain, and he released her. Regret clouded his eyes. Holding her side with one arm, she enjoyed the tickle of his beard under her hand again. She smiled, heat kissing her face again.

He started to say something, but her nose wrinkled, and he raced back to the meal before it burned beyond anything edible.

She closed her eyes and let her tongue trace each place his lips had conquered.

Chapter 47

"Let us try this today." Tio used more stripes of cloth to secure a stone to each foot. "Now practice lifting them as you have before."

Esmeralda gripped the edge of the bed and strained to lift one leg then the next. "I can't believe I have lost so much strength and mobility in such a short time."

"You have never eaten enough to keep your strength up."

She worked one leg several times before trying the other. Movement of her left leg pulled at her aching ribs, and she wrapped her arm around them for extra strength. "I didn't have much of an appetite."

He kissed her head as he moved to tend the fire. "I know the fault lies with me."

"I never said—"

"But 'tis the truth." He knelt, removed the stones, and put them in her hands. "I treated you terribly."

She raised one hand over her head. "The past can't be changed. I pushed before you were ready. Your fear kept you from showing how you felt. It does no good to revisit these things." She put one stone in her lap and reached for him. He came quickly, smothering her hand in his. "Tiobald, Second of Rustshade, Lord Sheriff, you are here now. Your love gives me strength and hope. I love you and always shall. I care not about what happened before. This," she kissed the back of his hand. "is all that matters."

He caressed her check, "How could I have been such a fool? You are a wonder." With a kiss to her head, he smiled. "Back to your exercises."

"No rest?"

"Nay, my good wife. You have rested long enough."

"I could do these things at home."

He shook his head and flashed a mischievous smile. "Not yet."

"What are you about?"

He kissed her cheek, "Regain your strength, Eszy, and you will see."

"You are a rascal." He chuckled and waved for her to continue her arm strengthening. But working her left arm at all only aggravated her tender side.

Just out of her reach, Tio stood with arms open wide waiting to embrace her. It took almost another week before she could stand on her own and walk these few steps required to cross the room. It tired her as if she had hiked up a mountain and the effort made her feel as though she would collapse. She fell into his arms and held on tight.

"Now we move outside," he said with a kiss.

"After a rest."

"Not until you get some fresh air." He pulled from her and left her standing on the far side the room. It would take an equal amount of effor to return to the bed or follow him a step outside the door. "I'm waiting, my love."

"Oh, you are a taskmaster."

"I learned well from the uncompromising woman I married."

She took slow, steady steps until she came next to him lacing their fingers together. He kissed her hand. The sun reflected in his silver eyes as he stared at her.

"Walk with me," he whispered.

"I'll go anywhere with you."

His thumb pointed back over his shoulder. "I think there are some willow trees not far from here. You said you needed more bark to aid with the pain."

She nodded, wrapped her arm around his for added support, and they slipped into the woods beside the hut. Leaves rustled under their feet. Sun filtered in a dizzying array of shafts through the thick canopy of new leaf growth. A hint of pine added to the damp earth that filled the air. She laid her head on his shoulder.

"Are you well?"

She reached her hand around his neck and pulled him down. "I'm with you." She pressed her lips to his. As always, his response was powerful and hungry.

She pulled away.

"Did I hurt—"

She placed her fingers over his mouth to quiet him. She turned her head, closed her eyes and listened. Mayhaps it was nothing. It'd been long since she'd been out in the woods. Weeks, months. A rustle came toward them. The smell followed quickly after. She touched Tio's arms. "Boar."

A deep long grunt filled the still air.

He scooped her up in his arms.

She gasped. "What are you doing? We need only make loud noises and make ourselves look bigger. They are easily scared away."

"The boar we have hereabouts are not so easily turned aside. We can't out run them with me carrying you. But I'll not leave you."

"That tree." She pointed to an oak with a large low branch. He charged toward it and hoisted her up as the drove burst from the undergrowth. A male and near a dozen sows with their young caught a scent. The adults' noses went up in the air. A couple of the younger ones ventured forward toward Tio, and returned to the others as Esmeralda found her balance. She reached a hand to help him up. But there wasn't time as the male, most of the sows, and several juveniles squealed, grunted, and charged at him.

"Tio!"

The predators and prey crashed through more brush, grunting and snarling like she had never heard. A human roar carried above it all.

"Tio!" Her screams ignited the fire in her ribs.

The pursuit faded. Only the last smatterings of the drove rutted not far from her tree. She couldn't get down without further injury, and she couldn't have out run them even at her best. Birds sang out in the stillness. She needed to find her husband. What if he was injured? She'd have no way to get him back to the hut.

The setting sun and fear made her tremble until she was sure she had rattled her ribs loose once again. She inched her way toward the trunk hoping, with its support, she could ease herself to the ground. Her thin gown caught and tore on bark. Pain filled every movement and each passing minute brought a terror of its own.

The remainder of the drove wandered away. The ground seemed an easy drop—if she wasn't so weak and already broken. She took a slow deep breath. The last rays of sun disappeared behind the trees. Once she got to the ground, did she follow the path Tio had taken or try to find the hut? Did she have the strength to do either? Tears burned. Crying would hurt more than breathing.

"Lord, 'tis not fair."

"What isn't fair?" Tio emerged from the shadows like some specter and she launched herself into his arms. She clamped her arms around his neck and bit her tongue against the pain.

His strong arms wrapped around her, gently stroking her back, and cradling her head. "Shh, Eszy. All is well. Don't fret, love."

She buried her face in his neck, breathing in his rich scent tinted with sweat. As her muscles relaxed in his hold, she trembled again.

"I'll get you back. Has been a trying day." He cradled her in his arms and she whimpered.

Beyond exhausted, she went limp. "I still need the willow. The pain is worse now." She dared look up at him. Cuts haphazardly marred his face as well as what she could see of his chest and arms. She brushed a few with her finger. "You may need some as well."

"Foolish of me to come in to these woods without sword or pike. I think every branch and bramble slapped and snagged at me as I fled. Every season, old Lucifer gets more injurious. Looks to have collected a gaggle of like-minded sows too." He gave her a gentle squeeze as he walked amongst the trees in the faint light of a rising moon. "Don't tell anyone, but I call the largest one Olva."

"Owe, that's a terrible thing to say," but she couldn't keep her snickers quiet.

"Here we are. Willows."

Esmeralda quickly collected what they would need before Tio carried her back. She was asleep long before they arrived.

Chapter 48

Tio's hand slid over her hip and up her side, stirring Esmeralda from sleep. Weeks of his care and good food saw her restored. She asked almost every day if they could return home. "Soon," was the only answer he ever gave. Eyes fluttered open to pale light leaking in the windows.

"Come," he rose and offered his hand. Outside, they circled the hut and moved toward the stream. "You have been asking for more than the wet cloth with which to clean." They stopped at a small pool. "'Tis not as warm as a proper bath, but not as cold as a mountain fed river either."

So that's why he smelled so good. He'd disappeared for a time yesterday on the pretense of gathering wood.

Her current gown lay tattered after the escape from the boar weeks ago. Tio pointed. "All awaits you." Garments and cleaning items sat on a boulder on the bank. He caressed her arms, and nibbled on the tender scoop of her shoulder. "Do you require assistance?"

Kissing his cheek she shook her head. "Soon," she mimicked. He laughed and swatted her behind as she walked away.

Though she couldn't see him, Esmeralda knew Tio was not far away. She, at long last, tore off the garments she'd been wearing since she woke. They were not salvageable at this point. The water nipped at her skin before she enjoyed its refreshing relief. The bath just before her marriage vows might have been this delightful, but she doubted it.

Dressed again in the purple gown he favored, wet hair soaking her back, and basket on her arm, she walked toward the hut. Tio stepped out from the tree he'd been leaning on. "Better?"

"Oh, was heavenly. Thank you."

He brushed her cheek in slow swirls. The center of his eyes expanded consuming the silver. His other hand slid around her waist. He kissed her forehead, brows, eyes, and nose before capturing her lips. Nipping at her bottom lip before he kissed her again. His kisses trailed along her jaw and down her neck. "I love the smell and taste of you." His words hummed over her skin.

Her heart thundered and skin warmed till she wanted to revisit the pool.

His kisses danced about capturing her lips and releasing them again and his hands roamed over her curves.

She took hold of his wrists and stilled him. Panting for breath and shaking with an unusual hunger, she rested her forehead against his chest until she could form words on her parched tongue. "Not here. Not in the place I came to die. Where I lay so sick for so long."

He kissed the top of her head and pulled from her grasp to wrap his arms around her. "As you wish." There was no anger or disappointment in his tone. Just agreement. "Let's prepare to go home."

They returned to the hut and gathered their few belongings. Esmeralda worked to detangle her hair before braiding it.

"Leave it down," Tio pleaded with a kiss to stay her hand.

"But 'tis not proper—"

He kissed her silent. "Your husband asks a boon of you, Wife. And no one would dare cast dispersions on the Second's wife—the wondrous healer of our entire shire." He captured her lips again making her dizzy. "For this day, your grand return, let your russet ribbons dance on the breeze. It will not be practical once you begin caring for an entire town of people. But, for today, favor me this request."

"As you wish," she whispered.

He smiled and kissed her soundly again. "Come, let us return." He offered her a package bound with a bit of string. Opening it she found a beautiful cloak.

'Twas your Christ Mass gift." He pulled back his own short cloak to reveal the tunic she had made for him. His eyes twinkled with desire, and her knees almost gave way. But he secured her gift around her shoulders, and taking her hand, led her out of the hut and toward home.

They had only walked a short distance before the sound of approaching horses danced on the morning breeze. Newt emerged from the trees with two additional mounts. "M'lady!" he called with such exuberance it sent the birds to flight. Rushing forward, he leapt from the saddle, knelt, and her kissed her hand. "All praise to the Lord for your recovery, m'lady. Sore it broke my heart to leave you here."

She pulled him to his feet. "Our God is ever faithful and merciful."

"Aye." A mischievous smile passed between Newt and Tio as the younger man gave a near imperceptible nod.

"What are you two about?"

Newt put out his arm for her. "Come m'lady. Your home awaits."

The saddle was not nearly as uncomfortable as during her journey six months prior, but neither was it delightful. Tio set a fast pace, and it took her a while to find a rhythm that did not provoke her nearly healed ribs. She wondered at his rush, but the memory of his hands caressing her and the sensations they stirred brought understanding.

They sprang from the forest and Rustshade came into view. The sun blazed through a sprawling gap in the wall. Nearly half the palisade was missing. Esmeralda reined in with a gasp. "Whatever has happened?"

Tio laughed. "Come, Eszy." They rode past the deserted shire. Not a person, dog, or sound lingered.

"Where is everyone?"

"Waiting." Tio urged his horse to greater speed, and she spurred hers to catch up.

"Waiting for what?"

Chapter 49

They continued to ride southwest of Rustshade, far from the gorge and the events that happened near there. Tio regularly alternated their pace between a jarring canter and a terrifying gallop that sent tears streaming back into her whipping hair. He reined in near a babbling brook and gave his horse its head.

"Newt, what have you brought to refresh us?"

The young man released his mount to drink the cool water as he rummaged in the sack slung behind his saddle. "M'lady's mead." He handed her a small skin. "Cheese, bread, and some dried meat." He offered the other items to Tio.

Esmeralda spent a few minutes walking and stretching her legs until feeling fully returned. "Where are we going?"

"Home," both men said as one.

"But Rustshade—"

Tio kissed her to silence. "The faster you eat, Eszy, the sooner you will know."

She ate her fill and started to braid her hair.

"You promised." Tio almost pouted.

"I only plait those hairs near my face. They whip in my eyes when you charge across the open areas and I can't see."

He kissed her hands when she finished binding the two thin strands together at the back of her head. "Shall we finish our journey?" Tio nibbled her jaw stealing her words and bringing an all-consuming heat across her.

She managed to nod and adverted her eyes from Newt. She very much desired her husband, but surely there was a better opportunity to display his affection than in front of the young man. Her tongue stuck to the roof of her mouth, and she reached for the skin.

Tio came up behind her, hands firmly around her waist. He kissed along her neck below her ear before he whispered. "I have waited too long to know you." With a gentle pull on her chin, he guided her face around toward him and devoured her lips. Every part of her ached for him.

"Then get me to wherever we are to call home, Husband. And quickly for you are being rather brash before Newt."

Tio chuckled and pointed to where Newt waited a good distance ahead of them.

A breath eased from her and the heat leaked from her cheeks.

Tio helped her into the saddle. "I didn't realize you could blush so, Wife."

"Treating ailing and injured men is one thing. Intimacy is something else entirely. One I know well, the other not at all."

He kicked his horse to speed, "Then it is time I teach you."

Esmeralda swallowed her heart and raced after him.

Descending a bit of a hill at midafternoon, a wagon laden with logs from the palisade rattled in front of them. As they drew alongside, Hubert and Garrett called out greeting. "My dear lady, glad we are to see you," Garrett said.

"Aye, a sight for these old eyes. Blessed be the One who restored ya. We have sore missed ya," Hubert added.

"Well, you both look quite hale." Esmeralda offered them a smile.

Garrett inclined his head. "Only because of the touch of your hand can we say, aye, m'lady."

"So, where are you taking the bits of Rustshade's palisade?"

A look shot from the two men on the wagon to Tio. She whipped around to catch the curt jerk of her husband's head.

Tio smirked at her with an arrogant raise of his chin. "They'll nay tell you either, but I cheer your clever attempt, Wife."

"Oh! Goose feathers to the highest heavens." She reined to a stop and crossed her arms.

They all continued. Tio didn't look back at her as called over his shoulder. "You'll never know if you insist on pouting there."

He was right, of course. But that only enticed her more. As they started up the next rise, she relented and spurred her horse to movement again.

Chapter 50

The sun painted the evening spring sky with vibrant golds, pinks, and purples. Esmeralda pulled her warm cloak tighter around her. Staying with the wagon had slowed them, and Esmeralda longed to be out of the saddle. Mayhaps she could ask Garrett to exchange places with her.

"Esmeralda, come!" Tio sat atop a rise ahead of her. His words rang out with the joy of a hundred birds.

She urged her mount forward and came abreast of him. She looked at him, but he was looking further beyond. She followed his gaze to a massive stone wall encircling the crown of the next large rise. The fortified rise sat within an expansive valley that was cut with a wide stream. Several fields lay plowed, ready for seed, surrounding the foot of the fortifications.

He flashed her a giddy grin, "Come!" He kicked his horse to full speed and called to her again. "Esmeralda, come!"

She charged after him. The wall grew as they approached. The crenulations of the battlements were still being completed as were the upper floors of the turrets. An incomplete spire poked above the wall for a time until they drew too near to see anything but wall.

A horn rang out filling the valley with its call. It was soon answered by another. The battlements filled with people—the inhabitants of Rustshade. They lined the top of the wall and stood on either side of the gate shouting and waving her welcome as Tio and Esz approached. They chanted her name interspersed with "Hazzah's". Tio ushered her ahead of him that she might enter the city first. He was soon lost to the crowd that crushed around her.

"Welcome home, m'lady."

"God bless you, m'lady."

"Sore glad we are for your return."

Above the din, came one squealed word. "Esz!" Jeni pushed through the throng and all but pulled her from her saddle. Crushed in an embrace only hampered by the growing bulge in Jeni's middle, Esmeralda struggled to breathe and her arms went numb. "Oh, how I have missed you, my friend."

"As I have missed you."

Jeni gripped her shoulders and held her at arms-length. "Let me have a look at you." Her gaze swept over Esmeralda from head to toe. "So help me, if you ever do that to me again…" Jeni gave her a shake and pulled her back into a full embrace. "Thank the Lord you are hale again. Bless His name."

Esmeralda didn't have time to catch a breath before Jeni released her, snatched up her hand, and started pulling her. "Come, you must see."

The crowd parted. The wall looked even bigger from inside, stretching back from the gate for at least a league. Foundations of homes lay in neat rows along forming streets. The blacksmith's forge looked complete as his home rose beside it. Two large structures sat at the heart of the town.

A huge church with its nearly complete spire faced east and the gate she'd just come through. Brother Joanis waved from the top step. "The good Lord bless you, Lady Esmeralda, as He has blessed us with your return."

"Where are we?" Esmeralda asked Jeni as they passed the beginnings of what looked like a tavern or inn.

"Haven."

"Haven?"

"Yes," Jeni giggled as she stopped in front of a long two-story stone and wood building beside the church. This building looked finished. "Our new home. All because of you."

"Me?"

"Yes." Jeni waved out her hand at the building as the crowd that had greeted her now pressed in close behind her.

No one said a thing. Did they all hold their breath? Esmeralda considered the building before her. The door was off-centered with one multi-paned window to the right of the door and four to the left. Above the door hung a square of wood carved and painted with a mortar and pestle.

"Welcome home, Eszy," Tio whispered coming up behind her.

"Welcome home, m'lady," the crowd sang out in a dissonant chorus around her.

Olva stood at the door with Mary on her hip. She smiled and offered a shallow curtsey as she pushed open the door. "Welcome home, Lady Esmeralda." Well... it *looked* like Olva.

Esmeralda walked through the door. A long wood counter sat in front of an entire wall of shelves only broken by a slim inset door. Bottles, jars, and bags labeled with the names of herbs, ointments and teas filled the shelves clear to the ceiling. Tears blurred them together in a puddle of joy.

"Do you like it?" Tio whispered.

A tear slid down her cheek but she could only nod.

To her left, Heart stood at the end of the counter in front of another door. She pushed the door open. Esmeralda walked past two windows and saw the town's people pressed against the panes.

The room she entered only continued a short way in front of her, but it ran the entire depth of the building to her right. An aisle divided the space. On each side, lay a row of narrow beds, a stool, and a short cupboard between each. She'd heard about hospitals from a traveling monk once. A frame hung with a fabric sat around each bed that could be closed for privacy. Washbasins adorned every cupboard. One sat open revealing bandages, towels, and a tin cup.

The tears danced down her cheeks as she passed a door to the outside on her left. More faces smashed against the many windows along this outside wall. A hearth sat cold at the end of the aisle. Kel met her at yet another door. Ido clapped as she held him.

Esmeralda clapped with him. "'Tis quite magnificent, is it not?"

The boy clapped and giggled, while his mum pushed open the door on her right.

Esmeralda stepped into the large room behind the shop-front. Long tables lined the walls and filled the space. Many were covered with scales and various sizes of mortars and pestles. A brick hearth with its chimney extending up through the ceiling sat in the very center, distributing heat around the room. Overhead, a dizzying array of drying racks hung. Most were filled with herbs in various states of readiness.

Jeni stood in the room as the windows on the back and right side of the shop filled with smiles. Jeni took hold of a rope, unwound it from an anchor on the wall, and allowed it to slip slowly through her hand. One of the racks laden with herb lowered before her so she could reach it.

Esmeralda covered the uncontrollable joyful sobbing. "I have never…" She choked on her tears. "'Tis wonderful."

Mutterings of "What'd she say?" peppered the glass panes.

"I love it!" she shouted so all might hear. "Thank you."

Cheers erupted outside and grew as her words were shared with others farther from the glass.

Jeni hoisted the drying rack back in place and secured it.

Tio came into view beside her, arms crossed and chest puffed up. "Truly? We did well?"

"Well? I have never dreamed of the like. 'Tis magnificent."

Jen clapped her hands. "Everyone had a hand in it. From construction, fabric for the bedding, leather for the aprons," she pointed to one hanging on the wall beside her, "the earthen jars, glass bottles, stoppers, flimsy tea cloth, rope and wood for the racks… we all did something."

Unable to do more, Esmeralda took her husband's and her friend's hands squeezing them tight. "Thank you." She released Jeni and waved at the thinning crowd through the windows. "Thank all of you."

They waved back.

Jeni spun on her heel. "Now, let's take you upstairs to see your home."

"*Ahhh.*" Esmeralda squeaked as she was snatched off her feet and clutched in Tio's arms. "We thank you for all your assistance, but I will be showing my wife the rest."

Beside the back door was a stairway. Tio carried her to the space that looked very much like their home in Rustshade, though larger. A cooking stove sat where the cutboard was located. The chimney from the hearth on the level below came up in the middle of the room to form the hearth in the wall between the living area and the main bedchamber. He pointed out three other rooms that filled the space, two with narrow beds, and one with a cradle.

Tio never slowed as he whisked her across the common room.

"Why so many rooms?"

"For all our children."

The fire blazed hot as Tio took her within the large bedchamber.

Chapter 51

"Are you happy?" Tio slipped his arms around her as she mixed an ointment in the back workroom.

She turned in his hold and wrapped her arms around his neck. "Happy? I am beyond joyful, awed, and full of wonder." She pushed up onto her toes and kissed him. "Thank you."

"Is there anything you require?"

"Not a thing." She brushed his lips again, savoring the taste of him, then turned back to her ointment. "MeeMa would never believe this is what became of me."

Tio came downstairs and handed her the heavy burgundy cloak. "Come, Eszy."

"Where are we going?"

He only smiled; the cloak perched on the end of his fingers. She put her fists on her hips, but it did no good. He stepped closer. Hovering over her lips but not kissing her, his warm breath danced over her skin. "Come with me."

Her skin buzzed with his nearness, and she couldn't resist pressing her lips to his. She took the cloak. "Does someone require aid?" He walked out the backdoor making her race to catch up. "How long will we be gone?" She followed him toward the makeshift corral next to the growing stables. Every building seemed to have a foundation, but most of the work on raising walls was focused on the inn, stables, and homes of the married couples.

Six horses were saddled, including her white mare and Tio's roan.

Connin inclined his head as they approached. "All is prepared."

The men were in the saddle before she even had time to gather up her reins. "Come, Eszy," Tio invited her with that mischievous smile.

Fighting with the fabric of her skirt and cloak, she settled at last and urged her mount to follow her husband. "We've only been home two handfuls of days. Where are we rushing off to?" She came abreast of him. A grin plastered on his face and chin held high. "What if I'm needed?"

"Jeni saw to the needs during your illness. She will manage until we return." He kicked his horse to speed and the other men followed. She looked to each as they passed, but they only shrugged or shook their heads. She followed her husband's example, and soon she rode beside him again.

They ate dried meat, bread, and cheese in the saddle at a slower place but didn't stop until the sun nearly touched the horizon. Esmeralda busied herself with the meal preparation while the rest of the men prepared camp. They would discuss any manner of topic except their destination. Because she stared into the sun all afternoon, all she knew was that they headed west.

Curled on the wide bedroll in Tio's arms, she tried again. He kissed her words away until she forgot all but his touch, his smell, and his taste.

The sun had barely lit the sky when he pulled from her arms. "If you wish to know our destination, then we best be on our way." He stepped from the tent disappearing in the faint light.

They nibbled on cheese while they broke camp and then mounted again. Tio set another fast pace. Though he slowed for the horses every hour, the rest of the time they charged across the land. A rise the shape of a large egg grew closer on their left. It looked like the one she could see from the battlements of Flatwell. Soon the stone walls around her childhood home came into view.

"Flatwell?" Why? Why were they coming again and with her? None of the women ever returned. Tio had said the Culling, or Blessed Choosing, would stop. She was the last to be chosen. But now that she had adverted the curse, had things changed? She turned and considered him as they perched on a rise within a grove of trees. Too soon, someone would see their approach and sound the horn. As always, maidens would form a line outside the gate as the town's folk held their collective breath praying their daughter might be kept from being spirited away.

Tio continued to stare at Flatwell. His smile was not as bright. "This is for you, my love."

"I don't understand."

"This town rejected you, mistreated you, and even threated to take your life." He turned, a mixture of anger and passion flashed in his eyes. "Today you return home, a revered healer of a mighty and growing town. The wife of the Lord Sheriff," he winked, "and one day ruler at my side. They will see the mistake they made." The last words growled and sent a shiver up her spine. "And today, we rescue one other from the abasement of this wicked village."

"Rescue…?"

"The one who taught and protected you."

"MeeMa?" The name squeaked.

"Aye." He reached for her hand. "Are you ready?"

"They will think…"

"We have come to *cull* again. I know. You, Connin, and I will ride into town." He raised his chin. "Raise your hood. We'll not let them know who you are until the opportune moment. Where will we find your MeeMa?"

A shiver danced over her skin, and she fought to sit still on her horse. "The wall encircles a small lake and a wooded area in the rear. She has a simple hut there."

He nodded. "Once we enter, lead the way, and we'll escort you."

"How are we to get MeeMa back to Haven? We brought no other horse, and I'm not even sure she can ride in her old age."

He spurred his mount forward. "The least the deplorable citizens of Flatwell can do is provide a wagon for her. We'll travel slower on the return. Like we did when we brought you to Rustshade."

The eerie call of the horn filled the plain.

Chapter 52

The line of trembling maids took their place outside the wall. A quick glance revealed Dinah was no longer amongst them. Her marriage to Vin must have taken place after all. Good for them.

Esmeralda, Connin, and Tio rode slowly toward the gate. "Return to your families. There will be no *Culling* this day or any other." Tio waved a hand for them to follow. Gasps and mutterings filtered on the air as Esmeralda rode through the main street toward the overgrown area where MeeMa hid.

Past the last home, she kicked her horse to more speed. "Connin can wait here." She called over her shoulder. "'Tis not much farther."

Heart thundering as loud as the pounding hooves, she wanted to urge her horse to more speed but didn't dare on the uneven ground and through the low branches. "MeeMa!" She called at the first sight of the thin wisps of smoke from the chimney. "MeeMa?"

She flung herself out of the saddle, brushed back the cowl, and charged through the flap door. The fire was low. A chill hung in the dank dwelling. Surely, she had to still be alive if there were even hot coals remaining. "MeeMa?"

She raced back outside and around the hut as Tio dismounted and collected the reins of her horse. "MeeMa?"

She caught a faint hum. A familiar hymn. MeeMa's favorite. "MeeMa?" She raced toward the sound.

MeeMa dipped a bit of soiled cloth into the stream. "Lord, my

Eszy's voice is clear to me this day. Bless her wherever Ye have led her. Oh, I sore miss that child, Lord."

"He has blessed me most mightily, MeeMa." Esmeralda brushed her arm.

It didn't seem possible that the woman could be shorter than last Esmeralda had seen her. MeeMa turned slowly. After staring for several heartbeats, her wrinkled hands rubbed over her eyes. "Can't be…"

Esmeralda wrapped her in a tight hug. "But, 'tis me, to be sure."

"Oh." MeeMa patted her back. "Oh, child." All other words bubbled incoherently on her tongue.

After a time, MeeMa released her and held her at arm's length. "Let me have a look at ya, child." She held Esmeralda's chin between her thumb and finger. "Ya've been ill."

She smiled. "You still don't miss a thing. Aye, I was near death. Water in the lungs and coughing up blood."

"No, couldn't be. No one recovers from such a state."

"The Lord restored me."

"How?" MeeMa's hands perched on her hips.

Esmeralda told her of the steam chamber Tio had created for her. "And, while I am loathed to tell him so, there might be truth in Tio's assertion that the foul cheese the men favor may have some healing powers. It is at least worth further investigation."

MeeMa squeezed her hands, "And who is this Tio ya speak of that makes yar entire countenance glow at the mere mention of his name?"

"Come, I shall introduce you."

MeeMa gasped when she caught sight of the man standing outside her home. "'Tis no man. Surely he is a brother of Goliath himself."

Esmeralda chuckled. Tio was a big man but nowhere near a fearsome giant.

As the women approached, Tio took a knee and kissed MeeMa's hand. Esmeralda had never seen him do that before. "Dear lady, I thank you with my whole heart for the love and knowledge you have poured into my Eszy."

Her other hand fluttered over her chest, "Aren't ya a fine gentlemen? 'Twas me greatest honor and pleasure. Might I ask though why ya have returned her?"

The grin filling Tio's face radiated joy. He rose and pulled Esmeralda to him. "We want you with us. Come live where you will be honored and respected. Where you will know comfort and peace."

"But what of Flatwell?"

"They deserve naught of you or our Eszy. And while my skilled healer wife can aid any other woman, she will need your help when she brings forth our children."

MeeMa considered her closely again. "Not yet though."

"Has not been for lack of trying, I assure you." Tio slapped at Esmeralda's behind before turning. "Collect anything you might wish to bring. I wish to shake the dust of this town from my boots as soon may be possible."

Esmeralda collected the few herbs she had yet to find around Rustshade. She hadn't had time yet to explore around Haven. MeeMa tucked a few mementos into a satchel and slung it over her shoulder. "Are ya sure we won't be needin' more than these?"

"You will not believe the home I take you to." Esmeralda looped her arm through MeeMa's. "I can't wait to show you."

They led the way back to the road, Tio bringing the horses behind. Connin waited for them with a small wagon. His horse was tethered to the back, and he bowed to MeeMa when she approached. "M'lady, might I take your burden and assist you into your chariot."

MeeMa shot a wink over her shoulder. "I favor these men ya have found, Eszy."

"They are a fine group," Esmeralda agreed as Tio kissed her and helped her into her saddle.

She pulled her cowl up again as they rode toward the gate. Tio's men had moved closer, remaining in the opening to prevent anyone from closing it or fleeing.

The town clustered together; many trembling. Dinah stood behind a man Esmeralda didn't know. She cowered from him, as he shouted for her to stay out of sight. A purple splotch adorned her face. Poor Dinah, she had adverted an imagined horror for a real one.

Connin drove the wagon with MeeMa through the gate as Tio turned to face the gathered crowd. "Citizens of Flatwell, take what comfort you can in knowing never again will the valiant and brave warriors of this fine Talgath kingdom visit you. You are wholly unworthy of our time or favor."

"And who might you be?" Flatwell's chieftain said. His vibrato added to the hand that rested on his sword hilt.

Tio and all his men opened their cloaks and drew their swords. Their tunics bore the royal crest. The people gasped and staggered back a step as if they had been struck a blow. "I am Tiobald, Lord Sheriff of Haven, Mighty Bear of the east, nephew and only heir of his Majesty Dunlang the Merciful." Tio nodded toward Esmeralda who sat slack-jawed beside him. "And this fine woman, you maligned, threatened, and brought much misery, is my lady wife, your future queen."

Her trembling hand would not pull the cloth from her head. One of the men beside her slid it back to her shoulders. The mouth of every person in the crowd gaped, as did hers. Slowly all of the men took a knee and the women curtsied low.

"Highness." The word came in an awed chorus.

"The Lord God Himself has clearly charged His people to care for the widow and the orphan. You did neither. Yet, even in the face of your hatred, God has blessed this woman with kindness and skill. As Talgath's Royal Healer, she will see to the instruction of all who wish to aid the sick and injured. But never will she aid this rat-infested hovel again.

"You can't take both our healers from us."

"As you have disdained them and their efforts, you are no longer worthy of them. Furthermore, not one man from this foul pit ever answered your king's call to arms to defend Talgath against its enemies. Pray the good Lord's protection, for the king will never come to your aid should the enemy knock on your door."

"How will we protect ourselves?"

"It no longer concerns me."

Tio looked to one of his men who pointed out Barid. Tio turned his sword tip to the quaking tanner. "I know the threat against my wife that came from your lips. May God judge you for your ignorance and cruelty."

Barid's head bowed. "He already has, your highness. Both my wife and daughter were lost during the winter."

Tio nodded, but Esmeralda clutched her hand to her heart as tears burned. "Even now, she still shows you compassion."

Father Abel stepped forward. "What are we to do when we need a healer?"

Tio motioned to his men, who began to file out of the gate to follow the wagon. "Pray you can arrive at the new royal city of Haven, and someone take pity on you before you die."

Before they cleared the gate, Tio called out three names. "Is there still a Wayne, Robert, and Bert here? Men of one family."

Bert and Robert raised their hands. "Aye, Highness, but our father, Wayne, passed this winter as well."

"I bring word from your sister, Olva. She is hale, well loved by a trusted member of my royal guard, and mother of a spry daughter she named Mary."

"Thank you, Highness."

They were some distance from the city when the word near exploded from her lips. "Queen?"

A boisterous laugh filled the glen and set the birds to flight. "Aye, *Your Highness*. We are slated to sit the throne when Dunlang, or the good Lord, deems the time is right. This is why we have been building the great city. Will be testament to the mighty power of the high king of Talgath."

Well this explained so much—his guard of her reputation, and his need to keep her safe from any rumor of taint. But, still, seemed this was something he should have shared before now.

"As a child, we were told of our king's fall to ill health. His hiding away, frail and weak, but still in command of a mighty army."

"You have met King Dunlang. Have you found him weak and infirmed?"

She shook her head.

"Threats from within our own court drove us to create Rustshade. A place to learn who we could trust and who was our real enemy. But after the death of his children, his wife, and his sister—my mother—leaving me as his only heir, he feared he was cursed. When all the women died in childbirth, he believed the curse to be true.

"Dunlang continues to meet with his council and generals. Both of us have led battles against those who, like you, thought Talgath was held by a frail hand. They have learned the error of their thinking, at great cost."

"But… me? As queen? Are you sure 'tis wise? I come from no family of import, an orphan and once feared witch."

He drew his mount so close to hers their legs were pinned between the creatures. He leaned close, cupped her cheek, and kissed her. "I would have no other at my side."

Afterward

"You should rest, my love." Tio's hands caressed the wide girth of her belly as she ground herbs for a tea.

Esmeralda leaned back against him and rested her head on his chest. "The only thing I need rest from is the kicking your son is doing to my insides." She moved his hand to feel the incessant prodding of the life within her.

Tio nibbled at her neck and nipped at her ear before his kisses skipped along her jaw.

The snap of fabric broke the silence, and Tio jerked.

"Leave the child alone, ya." MeeMa wound the strip of cloth around her hand and prepared to strike again. "Ya've done planted your seed. Let her bring forth one bairn before ya go planting another in her."

Tio held his hands up in surrender and chuckled. "No one, but you, would dare strike the sheriff and future king, MeeMa."

"Outside these walls ya can call yourself the pope, but here ya'll treat my Eszy proper or ya'll have me to answer to, boy."

Tio inched closer to her, bent, and kissed her on the cheek. "Well, if you forbid me my wife…"

The towel snapped again, but Tio leaned out of the way. His laughter filled the room. "Oh, ya rascal. Be off with ya. Surely the royal hall needs another pair of hands to see it raised before the rains set in."

Tio kissed Esmeralda's cheek.

"Out with ya!"

He bowed and disappeared out the door.

MeeMa clucked her tongue as she gazed in the direction he had gone. Her hand rested on Esmeralda's wrist and still her movement. She gave a little squeeze. "Ya have a fine one there, Eszy." She turned and touched her wide belly. "He'll be a good father and a good king."

"I believe so too, but what makes you think so?"

"He respects his elders, seeks after others who are wiser than himself," her wrinkled finger tapped twice on the tip of Esmeralda's nose, "and he does not think more of himself than he ought."

Their son, Adhemar, came into the world with relative ease a fortnight later. The first of five children Esmeralda gave Tio. Three sons and two daughters were raised in a time where children frolicked in the streets, and mothers called for them to come home as the sun touched the top of the walls. Tio was a good father, a mighty king, and a loving husband all the days of his life. Even as queen, Esmeralda tended the sick and injured, and trained the next generation of healers. Mary was her first apprentice of those born after the curse.

Glossary

Balyum – fictitious plant

Cenderberry – fictitious plant

Drove – a number of oxen, sheep, swine, or boar in a herd or group

Mead – an alcoholic drink made from fermented honey and water

Tonsure – the part of a cleric's head, usually the crown, left bare by shaving the hair

Trencher – a rectangular or circular flat piece of wood on which meat, or other food, is served or carved

About the Author

Michelle Janene (Murray) is a teacher by day and writes Christian fantasy and historical fiction in all her free time. She lives in Northern California with two crazy dogs and the characters of her imagination.

If you enjoyed *Culling a Miracle* please review it on your favorite site.

You can connect with Michelle on:
MichelleJanene.com
Facebook: Michelle Janene-Novelist or Strong Tower Press
Twitter: @MichelleJaneneM
Pinterest: www.pinterest.com/michellejanene
Goodreads: Michelle Janene
StrongTowerPress.com

Other Books

Check out these books also by Michelle

Mission: Mistaken Identity

The Changed Heart Series:
God's Rebel
Rebel's Son
Hidden Rebel

Seer of Windmere

Barbarian Hero

Guardians of Truth